Distant Starlight

Distant Starlight

Danielle Grift

Synecdoche Publishing

For information contact:
Synecdoche Publishing
synecdochepublishing.wordpress.com

Edited by Amanda Hovseth and Emily Burkey
Cover design by Tiffany Schank
Book design by Amanda Hovseth

ISBN: 978-1-945018-12-1 (soft cover); 978-1-945018-13-8 (eBook)

Library of Congress Control Number: 2018934303

First Edition: 2018

Dedication

The "Author and Perfecter of *Our Faith*" (Hebrews 12:2), my Mentor, and my Inspiration.

Immanuel, You are my Audience of One. May I always write with simplicity of purpose—to point others to You rather than to gain human attention (Colossians 3:23).

Prologue

He called her his Starlight.

Drew Leyton's heart burned. His sleepy daughter murmured softly, snuggling deeper into his embrace. Her head rested just above his burning heart; she was the reason shocks of pain rushed through it. Gently, Drew twirled one of Ariela's auburn tendrils around his pinkie finger.

For her murmur, he moaned. Was he really about to leave this sweet little girl fatherless?

"Daddy? Are you going to take me to see the stars again?" Ariela said.

Drew's eyes softened. For an instant the twinkle returned. The twinkle he accredited to his daughter, and never neglected to tell her so.

"Like the song!" Ariela would exclaim in a high-pitched giggle. "Twinkle, twinkle, little star…"

Drew buried his nose in his daughter's hair.

"My starlight." His voice cracked. "Not tonight."

Sweat beaded on his forehead.

He'd take her and her brother with him.

And hurt Marguerite even more? Drew shuddered. Wasn't this about Marguerite all along? Wasn't it about setting her free from the bondage called marriage? This is exactly what she wanted. She'd said so herself—to him, and to his brother. To Dallas.

Drew swallowed uneasily; what if Marguerite arrived home early? What if she changed her mind? Or resisted for the sake of duty? Or worse, watched him with an empty stare and guarded expression as he lugged out his things? He didn't have much time to spare.

And what if he did take the kids? No, then Marguerite would be forced to contact him. He planned to keep the same name and only move a few neighborhoods away—traceable and always in reach. The immense weight of these thoughts caused his insides to churn.

Ariela shifted slightly in his arms.

"My starlight," he tried to form the words, but his tongue felt leaded to the bottom of his mouth. Tears streaked down his face.

One last test. If she told him to stay, he'd stay. Forever.

"Do you want to sleep?"

Ariela nodded almost imperceptibly.

Had she so soon forgotten the stars?

And would he so soon forget his?

Numbly, Drew lifted his daughter and tucked her fluffy violet blankie around her body.

He padded to the door noiselessly.

"My Starlight," he whispered one last time. The door softly clicked shut behind him, enveloping his daughter in darkness.

Chapter 1

Joy on the Line

8 Years Later- Saturday, October 1st

Hastily, I untangled myself from the blankets which were twisted around my body. Yet, try as I might, I could not untangle myself from the suffocating darkness that weighed me down like chains.

Then I heard the rustling. Again.

That was it. Fear and desperation merged into a single hand and reached out for the lamp.

A floorboard creaked.

My heart rate doubled. Angst turned my fingers into clumsy sticks as I fumbled for the switch. *I just need to find the switch,* I thought.

A pair of clammy hands clamped on my shoulders. "Got—"

"Ahhh!" I screeched, frantically clawing the hands off my body.

"Ariela," the voice continued with mock sternness, "you did not let me finish— GOTCHA!"

*　　　*　　　*

"Looking back on it," I mused to Fahada, "I feel sorry for my brother. He hardly had time to glory in his victory before I punched him. Hard."

Fahada burst into laughter. Phone static reverberated

3

against my ears.

"Good for you!" She said through her chuckles.

I always loved her accented chuckle.

"If I were you I'm sure I would have peed my pants," Fahada said.

I snorted with laughter at the image this conjured. "Well… how about I just don't tell the rest of the story…"

Fahada clucked her tongue. "Ariela, what did you do?"

Hey, don't point fingers at me! It's you who has struggled with bladder control, not me."

I switched gears before our conversation could be hopelessly sidetracked.

"I need your help. How do you think I could get back at Al—" I paused. "Just a second here, let me check my closets. I'd hate for him to try the same trick again."

I bounced off my bed and quickly peered into each of my three closets. The first and third closet doors were wood, but a curtain replaced a door for the second. This had been Alexander's hiding place the night before. The shades of the wooden doors didn't used to match, so my daddy had covered them over with chalkboard paint for me—before he left. I brushed away the thought of my dad like a stray strand of hair falling over the eyes.

"Ariela, isn't Alexander, like, eight years older than you? You're so lucky that he still plays with you like that. I wish I had your brother."

I pounced on the word "still". "Exactly my point! He's twenty-four already. You'd think he'd be more mature by now!"

"Good luck," Fahada said. "He's a boy, you know. So, where do I come in, Ari?" Fahada pronounced the short form of my true name as if it rhymed with "Marie", as she always did. I credited it to her Arab accent.

"I need your help. I can't just let Alexander get away with something like this."

"Yeah, two heads are better than one. Besides, your brother is probably expecting payback—we'd hate to let him down. What's on your mind?"

My slippers slapped against the tiling as I paced up and down my bedroom. Fahada and I conspired together over the phone, our voices hushed and secretive.

"So, what would really annoy your brother? What does he hate?"

"The only thing that can garner a negative reaction from him is beans. He chokes on them like you did with the fish bone you swallowed when you came to visit us the other day."

Alexander and Dad used to be just like each other in the area of beans—in most everything, really. Alexander even started copying our father's lisp until it became ingrained in his everyday speech.

Fahada chuckled. "I guess that must have looked sort of funny when I started spluttering mid-sentence."

I snickered. "It was. Let's stay on topic, though. Is there any way we can implement beans into our plan?"

Both of us were silent as we contemplated.

"I have an idea. It involves paint." Her words were quiet and calm, in an almost sinister tone.

Following her train of thought, a sly smile gradually stretched across my face.

"Paint and beans, hmm. What a prime combination!"

It was payback time.

*　　　*　　　*

Two and a half hours later, I fingered a sample bean seed. The paint was dry. I grabbed a liberal handful and commenced the search for Alexander.

"I sent him to grab a couple onions from the garden," Mom said without looking up from the vegetables she was chopping.

"What are you up to?" My… uncle set down his knife and came over to give me a quick side hug.

I placed a finger over my lips and wriggled my left eyebrow at him.

"Ah." He nodded and smiled slyly at me.

I had always liked my uncle, but even after seven years it was still hard to think of him as "Dad".

A couple moments later Alexander walked into the kitchen, handed two onions to Uncle Dallas, and plopped himself on one of our white "spinny-chairs", as I called them.

"Have you been a good boy lately, Alex? Because, I have gifts for you!"

"Uh-huh? And what do you have that's worth receiving?" He turned his twinkling hazel eyes toward me.

Beans without the jelly. Your favorite.

I opened my left hand, revealing the "jellybeans". "Sweets for the sweet!"

"That's sickly."

I struggled to keep my face straight. Would he do it?

Alexander reached toward my palm.

I pulled it back. "Alexander! Your hands are gross! They're covered with mud."

"Oh." He wiped them off on his already-dirty pants.

"I hope you're going to change out of that."

He stared at me blankly.

"Right! I forgot! You don't know what 'change' means! But that's okay—I love you anyway."

"Yeah, right, like I believe that."

I wagged a finger at him. "Now, now. You better be

nice or you won't get any jellybeans."

Then I reopened my hand. Alexander carefully picked out the red and purple ones, neglecting the green ones.

In his mouth the "jellybeans" went, and then right out again.

"Ariela!"

Alexander lunged toward me. I dodged and raced for the patio door. I skipped all three steps on our deck and picked up speed to make up for my shorter legs. A grin stretched across my face as I heard Alexander yelling behind me, "You'll pay for this, Ari!"

I hadn't even made one lap around the house before he caught up and effortlessly swung me off the ground into his big, strong arms.

I squealed and uselessly tried to squirm out of his grasp, feeling absolutely like an immature little kid as I did so. Soon he let me down.

Breathing hard, I wasted no time in explaining. "That, my dear brother, was for the closet episode the other night!"

Alexander groaned before spitting out, "I thought you said, 'sweets for the sweet,' not, 'yuck for the sweet'!"

I tapped his chest for emphasis and pasted on a sugary smile. "You're as sweet as those jellybeans, Alex."

Alexander was my joy.

We reentered the house together, and together we plopped onto side-by-side "spinny-chairs". Again, we burst into a fit of laughter.

Mom dumped the pepper pieces from her cutting board into a large pot on the stove. She smiled a brief greeting at Alexander before returning to her work. If she sent a smile to recognize my presence, I didn't notice. That was normal—and okay with me. At least I had Alexander to pay attention to me.

"Kids, you should start getting ready to go for your visit," Mom said.

I regained focus quickly. "Right!"

Alexander and I had been invited to visit Fahada's Muslim family over supper.

"I'm so hungry I could eat an elephant raw," Alexander mentioned, patting his stomach. "I hope that Pakistani food tastes as good as ours."

I smirked at the irony. "If you can eat an elephant raw I'd be surprised if there's anything you wouldn't eat!"

The numbers on the microwave clock caught my attention, and I jumped to my feet. "Mom's right! I'll meet you at the door in 7.5 minutes."

I darted off to prepare. I played with my hair 'til it shined and made sure I looked impeccable. I had no clue what to expect from an Arab family, but I'd rather appear too formal than too casual.

When I arrived at the door, Alexander was waiting. "Seven minutes and 53 seconds, seven minutes and 54 sec—"

"Oh, never mind!" I wrinkled my noise at the sweaty smell emanating from his body and rushed outside. He could use the extra deodorant container in the car's side pocket.

Slowly and deliberately Alexander turned the key in the ignition, and just as slowly, the car rolled down the driveway.

"Speed up, will you? And here, put on some of this deodorant."

He removed his hands from the wheel to snatch it from my hand. The car jerked in a burst of acceleration.

I watched in shock as we careened toward the curb.

"Alexander! Turn, now!"

The bottle of deodorant dropped down his shirt as he returned his hands to the wheel.

We barely missed the curb.

"You can go a little slower now," I said meekly.

He happily obliged, and I didn't push the deodorant matter any further. Instead, I leaned back against my seat and practiced deep breathing the rest of the way to Fahada's house. By the time we arrived at their two-story brick house, I had mostly relaxed.

Feeling every rough edge of the stone pathway through my flats, I analyzed the house it led to. The old-style red brick lent it a near ancient appearance; but a cheerful flower bed against the house, with rusty-pink snapdragons climbing up a terrace and a carpet of sweet-smelling alyssum, brightened up the place.

Alexander raised the knocker and let it swing back against the grey metal door.

Seemingly the very moment Alexander let the knocker go, the door opened a crack and a cheerful, childish voice announced our arrival. "They're here! They're here! They're here!"

The door flung wide open and the little girl stared at us with huge, curious, dark-colored eyes. She smiled widely—almost gleefully—revealing a dimple on either cheek.

I couldn't help but smile back as I crouched down to her level. "What's your name, dear?"

"My name is Alia! It means 'from heaven' and I'm four!" Somehow, her smile grew wider as she spoke, as did mine.

Fahada came from around the corner and gave me a quick yet exuberant hug. She wore a hijab—the Islamic head covering for women. Not surprisingly, it was sparkly and colorful. Fahada opened her mouth to speak but was interrupted.

"Welcome!" Two middle aged women greeted us in unison.

"You can call me Aunt Javaria," the first said, placing a rebellious strand of hair underneath her burgundy-red hijab.

"And you can call me Aunt Layla!" the second added, smiling. She stepped forward and gave me a quick hug. She was the only woman without a hijab, her long hair was pulled back into an elegant "fish-tail" braid.

A young boy creeped out from behind Aunt Javaria's skirt.

"Ammi, I'm hungry." His voice contained a slight whine.

"Shh, Bassim, be polite." Then she looked up at us. "Come in! Supper's almost ready. Welcome to our home."

Alia snatched my hand and purposefully dragged me into the dining room.

"This is Uncle Sharik," Alia announced, "and this is my brother Omar—"

I hurriedly nodded and smiled at her uncle before letting my attention turn to Omar, and then her cousin Jawid—whom I recognized as Fahada's brother—and then to the next person... and the one after... until she had finished pointing out each of her siblings, cousins, and uncles.

Aunt Javaria cleared her throat. "We all have different tastes here," she said. "And we thought you might, too. That is why we have Pakistani, Canadian, and Mexican food on the table. There are forks and knives beside your plates, but also roti." She went on to explain how to use them and what each dish on the table was made up of—

they had definitely prepared a feast!

As we ate, conversation started to bubble forth from all directions. "Uncle" Sharik engaged Alexander, and many joined in the conversation as well. I used the opportunity to whisper with Fahada, who sat next me. As I turned toward her, I caught Jawid's stare from next to her.

"What is it?" Fahada asked, giving me all the support I needed.

"Well... obviously, since your Aunt Layla isn't wearing a hijab, it is acceptable for you to not wear one, and you don't wear one at school, so then why—"

"She doesn't?" Jawid asked quietly.

"I figured you wouldn't mind, Jawid?" Fahada hesitated.

Jawid shook his head. "You know what I think. We'll talk more later."

What? Does her brother control her life? I remembered what Fahada had said a while before: 'I wish I had your brother'.

"Tell me, dear, how has school been going for you lately?" Aunt Javaria asked, distracting me. Soon, swept up in many delightful conversations and stories, all disturbing thoughts of Jawid disappeared from my mind.

"You've certainly outdone yourselves," I said finally, my words bringing the evening to a close. "The food was absolutely delicious and well-prepared, and I couldn't have imagined better company. Truly, thanks so much for inviting us!"

Cheerful replies of "no problem", "our pleasure", and "come again!" answered me.

I stood up, and one-by-one the rest followed, making a large procession toward the door.

Alia slipped through the throng of people and hugged my legs. "Will you come again? Please!"

Everyone laughed.

"We'll see, but I'd love to, Alia."

Both aunts offered me a warm hug, and I wished I had more words to thank them for their hospitality.

Alexander shut the door behind us.

I let him pass me by, and took the opportunity to gaze up at the millions of bright stars dotting the wide expanse of sky.

The door reopened, and Fahada crept out to stand beside me, asthmatic puffer in hand.

"I'm sorry about Jawid. Lately he's been doing… some heart searching, I think, and in his search for meaning… well, enough said."

"No need to apologize, it's not your fault. But, if you want to talk there's always Monday."

I plodded down the stone path and climbed into the car. "This time, Alexander, don't drive so fast!"

His brief nod acknowledged my comment. "Ari, I forgot to phone Pastor Garth back; I said I'd call him tonight."

"Oh, don't sound so woebegone, Alexander. Did you tell him you'd call at a certain time?"

"No, but he tried calling an hour ago, and I missed it."

"Just tell him you were witnessing to Muslims," I said.

"Don't kid me right now, Ari. I want this job! I don't want him to think I'm irresponsible."

"So, you're planning to accept the offer?" As soon as the words left my mouth, I realized that I was hoping he'd turn the church down, the church in Alberta—more than 300 miles away.

I lowered my head.

"Of course!" He said. "I've been trained for this, and I've prayed about it. It's a perfect opportunity to be a youth pastor and associate pastor."

I knew all along this was going to happen. But, this actually was happening.

"What's the use of being close to my brother if I won't even be able to see him?" I peered out into the dark streets, biting my lip to keep the tears back.

"I thought of that," Alexander said. "That's why I'm going to ask if I could have a little more time to get ready first."

My attention snapped back to him. "How much time are you planning to ask for?"

"They're in a bit of a tight spot right now, so I'd say two more weeks."

At least it was longer than Dad gave me.

Alexander drummed his fingers on the steering wheel. "If they don't go back on their offer."

"Hey, don't be so uptight," I said mildly.

Alexander simply rolled his eyes in response and ruffled my hair.

"Two hands on the wheel, please," I said.

Chapter 2

The Hated Hollowness

Skillfully manipulating my tongue, I rolled a piece of spearmint gum across the roof of my mouth. I fished it out to inspect its state before popping it back in for another round of agitated chewing.

Fahada walked beside me with the hint of a skip in her step. Even her tongue maintained a pattern as it wagged incessantly.

We halted by the finger-smudged glass door to St. Joan's Ice Cream Shop. I chewed harder, working all remaining juice out of the piece of gum.

"Are you going to answer my question?"

I couldn't ignore those puppy-dog eyes and swallowed the gum. "Sorry, friend. I should be focusing more on you on your special day."

Fahada grinned. "Forgiven. Should I try the bubble gum flavor or cookies and cream?"

"Bubble gum. I'll take cookies and cream." It was how I always replied; no use switching things up now.

I swung open the door and executed a sweeping bow.

"You first, mademoiselle."

The lone ice cream attendant topped up a cone before calling to us. "Hi, ladies! The normal?"

As usual, Lilac's pleasant smile lit up her face, but it was someone past her who caught my attention.

With windswept sandy-blonde hair and a tall stature, Woodlynd stood out from his Asian companions. He had always been the friendly type who could mix and match with any group of people. Maybe that's why I had considered Woodlynd my best friend in middle school.

Woodlynd caught my stare and, as nonchalant as ever, flashed me his trademark wink.

"Um, yes, bubble gum and cookies and cream—the normal," I said quickly.

Fahada nudged me gently. "I just told her that."

A flush swept across my face. "Oops."

With no extra delay, we held the cones in our hands.

"Enjoy yourselves now," Lilac said pointedly to me. "But don't have too much fun," she teased towards Fahada.

"Thank you!" I said and made a beeline for the corner table.

Fahada nudged my shoulder. "Do you think she's close to the right age for Alexander?"

I sat down before answering quietly, "It never occurred to me—good call!"

I zoned in on devouring my ice cream, trying to drown out distracting thoughts of Woodlynd.

"Mmm, the bubble gum flavor is SO good," Fahada said.

"It matches your personality—very colorful."

"And different… a little abnormal," Fahada added.

"Yep."

"Hey, you weren't supposed to agree!" Fahada smacked my arm with her free hand.

With Fahada's sudden movement, the top scoop on her

cone slid off and landed on the table with a plop.

I snickered. "Serves you right!"

"I dare you to lick it off!"

I decided to distract her. "So, Fahada, how are you planning to celebrate your birthday today?"

Fahada chomped on the bait with exuberance. "We'll have lots of good food: cookies, sesame sticks, cakes—they're called gateaux—and french bread sandwiches! And I bet that while I'm gone, my cousins will decorate the house with zeena! I think you would call those paper garlands… Um, and yeah! That's it." As suddenly as her words had begun, they came to a screeching halt—not a rare occurrence for eccentric types like her, I decided.

"So…" I started slowly. I licked the drips slipping down the cone. "You're in a better mood today? When you and I left off you were, well… off, about Jawid."

"Mm-yeah. He's a bit of a deep thinker."

"There's nothing wrong with that, I'd say."

Fahada scrunched up her face. "It just seems so fast. When we immigrated five years back I instantly embraced the new culture, new food, new sights—and less religious rules. Our relatives didn't really care, and I found out Dad didn't either. We still traveled to the mosque every week—but that was it. Jawid, he didn't like it. He said that there should be more, and he was going to find it. He's been studying the Koran and the Hadith until late at night. He hasn't found peace, but he has found purpose. He's really dedicated to this being-a-Muslim-thing, and he wants me to be as well."

"He seems quite overbearing."

"Perhaps. Restless, too."

She cast her listless stare out into the distance, like a hook flung far into the ocean. Her eyes narrowed, and I knew the lure had been snagged—her attention hooked. Instinctively, I followed her gaze all the way to the stucco beige wall. That was as far as I could see. And then it occurred to me that a wall was all she saw, too.

Disturbed, I set down my half-devoured cone and grabbed my friend's hand.

I caught a glint in her eye, a shimmer of tears reminiscent of the glistening upon water at sunset. The backing in her eyes dissolved, collapsing with the finality of a tsunami. The shallow sheen vanished into an ocean's gently lapping waves. The calm before a storm, I knew.

With that same force of loaded calm, Fahada focused her eyes on me. I shuddered, taken aback. I hated the hollowness I perceived within their depths.

"I want my brother back."

"And I want you back." My voice was confident, not letting on to how unnerved I felt. "And I will get you back!"

I wanted to see that sparkle of joy lighting up her face like a string of Christmas lights, that all-so-familiar face that I had grown to love.

Be it containing a glimmering puddle or an ocean, the rim of Fahada's eyes overflowed.

"No, Fahada, no! It doesn't need to define you, Fahada! I mean, he doesn't need to define you. Wipe those tears off your face and plant your smile back on it. I want to see you happy." I placed a comforting, though sticky, hand on her shoulder. "And maybe one day you will get your brother back. Did I tell you about my brother's plans?"

My words felt shallow and abrupt.

"No. Tell me," she said anyway.

"I want my brother back, too," I told Fahada. "He's planning to leave for Alberta, to work at a church there."

"Mm."

"I'm thinking—won't any church do? Why in Alberta?"

Fahada spoke slowly, as if weary and fatigued. "The difference is, your brother's not too far gone. He hasn't left yet."

"His heart is there already, though, and it pains me."

"Tell him that. Maybe he'll understand more than you think," Fahada said.

She smiled and placed a comforting, though sticky, hand on my shoulder—much like I had done.

"I will," I said. "I will."

Above her tear-streaked cheeks, an expression in the form of a twinkle reappeared in Fahada's eyes. "I dare you, dear friend," she said.

Chapter 3

Then Don't Go

Throughout the rest of the afternoon I mulled over Fahada's words. I would change my anthem to "I want my brother to stay" instead of "to come back". It was an act of strategy. To take up a solid position deep in the heart of territory you wish to overcome. Then, even if the area is already captured, upon retreating you will still be left upon a certain amount of coveted ground. I couldn't make my brother stay, I knew, but maybe a compromise could be arranged.

Fahada just laughed at my theories, which I shared on the walk home.

"You most definitely spent too much time on that World War II history paper!" Fahada pointed out.

I shrugged, deciding against sharing that I only got a 'B'.

Fahada and I parted ways by Griffin Lane, and the rest of the way home I was free to think as I wished.

I felt like a robber sneaking into an eerily quiet house, but I ignored the feeling. I settled myself down on the couch and continued to strategize.

After a few minutes, I pulled out a magazine that had slipped between two couch cushions. It was a fishing magazine. I set it on the coffee table beside me and then got up to open the window a crack—this way I could hear Alexander when he came home.

Soon enough, I detected the growing rumble of a diesel engine. A school bus passed by and, behind it, my brother's Chevy.

A moment later Alexander lumbered along the short pathway, iPhone pressed against his ear with one shoulder.

The door pushed open. I darted down the hallway to stay hidden and listened to his conversation.

This was it. It was Pastor Garth.

I slipped further into the hallway and disappeared into the office.

As I leaned on the door, Alexander's excited voice came loud and clear, "Thank you, Garth! It's all I can say. Yes, two weeks Saturday."

I could nearly see Alexander's hands waving about as his long strides carried him back and forth across the living room.

Alexander lowered his volume, but I could still pick out his final good bye.

I took a deep breath and stepped out.

"It's final?" I asked, walking up.

Alexander grinned widely and swung an arm around my shoulders.

I shrugged it off. I didn't want to share his excitement. I pushed my forehead into his shoulder—I just wanted my brother.

"What's wrong, Ari?"

I gritted my teeth as my tears fell. This wasn't the timing I had expected.

"Ari, don't cry!" Alexander pulled me into a hug. "What happened?"

"You becoming a Christian happened." The clear tone of my words surprised me. "You going to seminary happened. My brother about to leave me is happening."

"You know I'm not doing this to hurt you, right?"

I struggled to explain and pulled back. "What I know is very different from what I feel, Alex."

Through blurry eyes, I watched his shoulders slump.

I wondered who was hurting the most now, but reminded myself he was still the one leaving.

Alexander just shook his head, as if confused. "I'm sorry, Ari. I'll miss you. I really will!"

"Then don't go."

*   *   *

Tuesday, October 4th

I awoke before my alarm from a night of tossing and turning. I didn't feel much better now, either.

Brushing away frizzy hair that had fallen over my face, I plodded to the bathroom.

As I entered, my reflection in the chinked mirror caught my attention. Normally, I would have smirked at the bed-headed face staring back at me, but today I was in no mood for humor.

Undecided between brown and black, straight and curly, my hair fell drably to just below my shoulders. My hair was too dull, my pimples too many, my face too pale, my nose too small, my eyelashes too light. I picked up a container of foundation that showed no evidence of previous use. Carefully I swiped foundation over the couple of glaring red pimples on my chin and nose, proceeding then to cover the rest of my face with a light layer of it. Next, I took hold of the lipstick; then, eye shadow, eye liner, mascara, and blush. Earrings went in.

My hair transformed into a French braid. I practiced a smile.

Why? Why did Alexander have to become a Christian? Why does he have to leave?

And then it hit me—he was just like Dad.

I leaned my elbows on the counter to study my eyes: one amber, one green. It had taken me a few years to notice, as the difference was not distinct.

When I first asked, Mom told me it was because of a disease I had as a baby, resulting in my left eye containing more pigment than the other.

I liked Dad's idea better. He had said, "One from me and one from Mom!"

Dad always used to tease me about my eyes—no, not about the color—but at how he need only take one glance at my eyes to read my thoughts.

And he had compared them to the stars. On the evening of my fifth birthday, at 11:02 PM, Dad had snuck into my bedroom. I had awoken instantly to his soft voice, asking me to get up. I still remember the sense of adventure rising inside of me as we tip-toed down the stairs, unlocked the front door, and padded, barefoot, onto the front lawn. An oddly shaped instrument stood there, illuminated by the moon. Daddy had adjusted the telescope for me, and said, "Take a peek!" With one hand on my back and the other on the telescope, Daddy had patiently pointed out different stars and constellations.

After a few minutes of staring in wonder at the millions of bright lights, I had spun around to share my excitement with my dad face to face. Then my eyes had widened even further with delight. "Daddy," I had said. "There are stars in your eyes!" I had referred to the twinkle in his eyes, highlighted by the special lighting.

"And in yours, too," Daddy had reminded me. He had wrapped his large arms around me and pulled me in. "You're my little starlight."

I jerked; that single line reminded me of many good times, and many late-night snuggles. But, I hadn't heard those words in eight years.

Three tears slid down my face, smearing my mascara.

That was my first clear indication that this day wouldn't be one of my best. As I turned to go, another quick glance in the mirror revealed my pitiful, red face—prompting a fleeting wry smile.

Chapter 4

Unanswered Questions

As I concentrated on Mr. McDiarmid's description of DNA strands, I placed my feet on top of each other for increased warmth. My position in the far corner of the class, right up against a vent which was blowing cold air on my ankles, had not been a wise choice.

Mr. McDiarmid took one brief glance at Thomas (the studious one), who had begun to bob his head, and burst into an even more extended monologue.

It took all my self-control to restrain a groan. I was absolutely confident that Thomas was nodding for an altogether different reason than our teacher had assumed.

The girl next to me, Jade, smiled condescendingly at me before delicately picking up her pencil with newly-manicured fingers.

Fahada made a face at her from across the table, boosting my spirits just a tad.

I picked up an empty loose-leaf paper and wrote: Still think Woodlynd's a fitting match for me? Even with his new haircut?

I pushed hard on my pencil, and sure enough the lead snapped.

"Fahada," I whispered. "Do you have a writing

utensil?"

As I took the pencil from her hand, I discreetly placed the paper in hers. She read it and playfully stuck out her tongue at me.

"Later," she mouthed.

We were the first out of the classroom doors once we dismissed.

I nudged Fahada. "So, what do you say?"

"Just a second," she said, pulling out her puffer. "This classroom always makes my asthma act up—too stuffy."

"Must be the teacher," I muttered.

Jade swished past us, an overbearing whiff of floral perfume settling in our nostrils with burning heat. "Nice make-up," she called over her shoulder, "trying to attract someone's attention?"

I clenched my fists, waiting for Fahada to burst out in my defense. Instead, Fahada burst into a coughing fit and once more retrieved her puffer.

I turned my attention back to Jade, watching helplessly as she practically sashayed up to a tall, carefully sculpted someone—Woodlynd. She said something that I couldn't make out, and he laughed. His smile seemed too big, too real.

"Didn't see that coming," I said.

Fahada placed her puffer back inside a purse pocket. "Do you remember when Jade and her side-kick Kylie made fun of me when I first switched to this school? I—"

"Fahada, I don't really care right now."

Fahada's head jerked toward me, and she scanned my face.

Placing a hand on her hip, she said, "Now, what's with that attitude?"

Her smile didn't brighten up her face like it normally

did.

It took effort for me to shift my stare off Woodlynd and onto Fahada. "It's just been an overwhelming week, okay?"

"Okay," she answered in a small voice.

I sighed, feeling small myself. Was brooding over a guy I no longer knew worth hurting my friend? "Let's hurry to the next class. Ms. Kroeker doesn't take to tardy students." I stepped forward. "Afterward, I'm walking home by myself. I need a break from all this."

Moments later, a tiny, bumpy package was gently wedged between my fingers. My face crumpled as my fingers curled around the Oh Henry bar, my favorite chocolate treat.

Fahada never missed a step as she silently re-zipped her purse.

*   *   *

My loaded backpack jostled roughly against my back as I burst into a sprint. I clutched assignment instructions and a few pages of loose leaf paper tightly in one hand. I didn't want to risk letting the pages be trampled by the classmates and strangers spilling out of the doors behind me.

I slowed to a jog by the freshly grated road and checked over my shoulder. The cluster of people reminded me of a hive of swarming bees. Once more, I gathered up energy for another sprint. This time I only let my legs rest when my lungs reached capacity.

Sucking in air, I readjusted my backpack. I let my eyes absently wander across the rows of small but well-kept houses. I passed a sky-blue paneled house, glancing in the window to discover a calico cat watching my every move.

The moment of peace soon passed as I let my thoughts

flood back into the forefront of my mind.

What is with my attitude? Why am I covering up my love for Alexander by emphasizing the pain he will cause me? Why do I value a boy over my friend? Every word that leaves my mouth hurts the people I love. Is love of myself clouding my vision?

I stumbled on a fist-sized stone. A well-aimed kick sent it flying. I exhaled.

What am I even doing with my life?

With one sideswipe of my foot, a handful of pebbles skidded off onto the road.

And, what of Woodlynd?

No one—not even Woodlynd—really considers me beautiful. Not beautiful enough, anyway.

I booted another pebble.

The purr of a lawnmower alerted me again to the presence of people, but I paid no attention.

There isn't a single person that actually loves me! Not even my brother.

I knew it wasn't the full truth, but I was too far in to refute the lie.

Soon Alexander will leave me.

I stopped in my tracks, and the blood in my veins paused with me.

"And this one too!"

The pebble soared.

Out of the corner of my eye, I noticed a page slipping off my stack of books. Frantically, I tried to snatch it before it fell, but my upraised leg put me of balance. I teetered for a moment, then crashed to the side-walk.

My hands released the rest of the stack an instant before they scraped along the rough cement.

The motor of the lawnmower choked and was silent. I sat up and snatched a paper floating toward the road. My hand smeared blood across the page.

The sound of footsteps drew near.

"Are you alright?" A soft, concerned voice asked.

"I'm okay."

I focused my attention on the young woman before me. With her sweet smile, delicate form, and soft eyes, she felt strangely familiar.

"You sure you're okay, Ariela?" She asked, looking me straight in the eye.

Lilac. The nice lady from the ice cream shop.

"You look like you need a hug," Lilac said.

Something in me caved—I leaned into her warm body and started to cry. Like, really cry. Once the tears started to fall, they wouldn't stop. My whole body began to wrack with painful sobs. It felt good in a weird sort of way.

Lilac wrapped her arms around my shaking body and just held me. As I remained there in her embrace, I felt wall after wall after wall in my heart crumbling. I felt sick but couldn't throw up. I was sick of myself, and I was sick of how I had been treating others.

After several moments, I let go of Lilac. Tears glimmered in her eyes and on her cheeks, too.

"I have to go," I said reluctantly.

"I'll walk with you, just let's first gather your things."

"Oh, you don't have to!"

Lilac shook her head. "But I want to!"

And, so she did.

Five minutes later, Lilac waved good-bye while I stood on the thresh-hold of my house. One hand rested on the door knob, my other hand clutched Lilac's personal Bible—a present for me. In just a few short minutes she had convinced me to give reading it a try.

"It'll offer you the answers you seek," she had said.

If only something would.

Chapter 5

Last Minute Matchmaking

I set down my fork. "You'll call me when you get there, right?"

"Dude, don't worry about it," Alexander said. "You know I love you."

I raised an eyebrow. "What's with 'dude'?"

"Sorry, I meant 'sis'."

I let my teeth snag on my bottom lip, while Alexander carelessly sprayed spaghetti sauce all over his face with each mouthful of supper. "But, is there anything that could change your mind?"

"No, you'll always be my little sis." He stuffed a couple more fork-fulls of spaghetti into his face, changed his mind about chewing, and said, "Sis, my mind is made up. But, if you want, we can talk more later."

"A lot of later that we have," I grumbled.

"All the way 'til tomorrow morning."

As I handed him a napkin, a thought popped into my mind—a connection I had already made earlier. *It probably won't keep him from going, but still… it will be a meeting worth orchestrating. For the sake of romance.*

"I think we should do something special—just the two of us—before you leave. Maybe we could go out for ice-cream?" I said.

"How about for dessert?" Alexander agreed instantly.

"Um, sure. I'd better work quickly." I slapped my hand over my mouth.

Thankfully, he didn't catch it.

I pulled out my phone and scrolled down until I found my most recently added contact.

Alexander and Lilac. Definitely sounds better than Woodlynd and Jade!

"And Alexander, I think this time I'll drive."

This time, it didn't take much to push my brother out of the door.

Alexander grabbed the door handle. "That Reese's Pieces twister is calling my name!" He paused for a brief moment by the door, then swung it open to let me step through.

"You sure about driving, Ari?"

"Of course. I'd prefer to arrive in one piece."

Alexander and I relaxed in comfortable silence during the five-minute drive.

Even before we entered the little ice cream shop, loud voices and laughter seeped through the thinly insulated walls.

Alexander noticeably straightened. Not bothering to look around or adjust to his surroundings, he merged into the line immediately inside the doorway. It wasn't that the line was long, just that the area was quite cozy.

I began scanning the area, searching for faces I recognized. From across the room Lilac's hand shot up in a wave, and I motioned for her to come over.

I gave her a quick hug.

"Hey, how do you know Lilac?" Alexander asked me. "I thought *I* was the most frequent visitor here!"

Alexander firmly shook Lilac's hand.

"Yep." Lilac nodded with a straight face. "You certainly have developed a stable and long-standing relationship with this place."

Alexander laughed boisterously.

"I guess that makes sense," I mused. "Somehow it didn't occur to me that you'd know each other, too."

Lilac smiled pleasantly, passing a glance to the opening door. In the meantime, Alexander placed our order.

Lilac brought her attention back to Alexander. "Ariela and I met each other on her walk home from school a little while back. She said you're moving away...tomorrow, is it? Where to?"

This wasn't my favorite topic, but at least she was showing interest in Alexander. I watched his face with avid curiosity as it lit up.

"Beaumont, Alberta. I've actually been hired on as a youth pastor and associate pastor at Magasin Avenue Christian Church."

"Oh, really?" Lilac blinked and tilted her head. "Ariela mentioned that you were a believer, but I didn't know..."

"To what extent?" Alexander said for her as he handed me my cone. He grinned widely. "So, I'm pretty pumped about this change!"

I attempted to keep a neutral look on my face.

Lilac laughed lightly. "Right. I'm a Christian too, so I can understand how exciting it would be to receive a new ministry position like that."

Alexander paused with a spoonful of ice cream up close to his face. "You're a Christian too? Neat!"

Lilac beamed then made eye contact with each of us. "I've enjoyed this conversation. Thanks for saying hi! I'll have to excuse myself, though, it's family evening at home."

"Wouldn't be a bad idea for us either. I should probably share my brother with my parents." I jabbed Alexander with an elbow and glanced toward the door.

Alexander pulled it open for Lilac. "Thanks for the chat, Lilac!" He then turned to me. "Go ahead."

I did, but then said, "I thought we were going to stay a little longer yet—I mean, Mom and Uncle Dallas won't even be home for another fifteen minutes or so."

Alexander followed me to the car. "Why did you glance at the door then?"

This time I whispered. "I just wanted you to open the door for Lilac."

He shrugged. "Well, we could go back in for another ice cream, if you want."

I thwacked his shoulder and laughed. "All good, Bro. Let's go home and set up a board game. Unless you need to finish packing."

"I'm all for a round of Risk! Throw packing out the window." Alexander grabbed the dial on the radio and cranked it up.

The smile drained off my face. A game of Risk? This would make for a long evening.

Two hours later I finally crawled into my bed, snatching a pen and sheet of paper as I did so. With my blankets wrapped tightly around me, I let my gel pen float across the page.

□□□□ □□□□□□□□□,

I fought against my heavy eyelids and yawned. Even my pen felt weighted as I tried to form my thoughts. I scrawled out a few more words before letting my pen rest.

* * *

Abruptly I sat up, a sudden sound disturbing my sleep.

I stumbled out of bed and headed toward my closets. Waving my hand about inside of them, I discovered nothing out of the usual.

I quickly turned the room light on and returned to search for my letter. Upon discovering it halfway under my pillow, I lovingly picked it up and began to straighten out its wrinkles.

"Dear Alexander," I read aloud. "Do you remember how when we were very little, every time I would pinch you or say something mean (which was quite often) and I would say 'I love you' afterward? Finally, you told me that you would only believe I loved you if I said, 'I love you!' two hundred times in a row. You thought you had my little six-year-old brain stumped. I tried. I really did try. And now I'll try again.

"I love you. I love you! I love you. I love you!"

With my stomach in a tight knot from sadness, I picked up where I left off, writing—and counting—well into the night.

Chapter 6

When Breathing Gets Tough

A floorboard creaked, but my eyelids barely fluttered. The late evening the night before had done me in.

Large hands grasped my shoulders and shook them gently. "Wake up, Ariela, I'm leaving now."

"What time is it?" I asked groggily, wiping sleep out of my eyes.

"It's 8:30. Time for a goodbye hug before I leave," Alexander said.

I was quiet for a moment, but pulled myself to a sitting position.

Alexander gave me a quick squeeze. He smelled like shaving cream.

He started to leave.

I rubbed my face once more. There was something I was forgetting.

"Alexander, you'll call me when you get there, right?"

"Sure," he agreed, shutting the door softly behind him.

I sank back into my bed. When I next rolled over, it was 9:30. *Shoot.* As I readjusted, something crinkled underneath me, reminding me of the times I had to crinkle up newspaper to start a fire.

I blinked hard. Disappointment mingling with a sense

of 'blah' as I realized Alexander was gone and I hadn't even given him his note.

Maybe he wouldn't have cared anyway.

I hesitated for a moment, then crushed the paper into a ball in my hands and tossed it over my bed-stand and into a garbage can.

I stumbled out of bed to ensure it reached its target. It did.

Now, to start a life without my brother. I pressed my eyes tightly shut and breathed deep. Time to move on—I was scheduled to be at Fahada's house in half an hour to help her babysit her younger cousins.

I flitted around our littered rec room, snatching puzzles, movies, games, and books from the shelves, floor, and in-between couch cushions. I piled as much as I could into my backpack and zipped it shut with an air of finality.

I trekked to Fahada's house with a forced smile on my face. I decided I would choose to be happy—to focus on the immediate present, and not the void Alexander had left behind. I chose to let my heart dance along with the colorful leaves swirling from the tree tops to my feet. I chose to imagine the sing-song tone of Alia's voice, lifting me to a place of light-heartedness. I chose to be grateful for the babysitting opportunity and for some friend time with Fahada.

I sighed resignedly, envisioning the pile of homework forgotten on my bed stand—due tomorrow. *Too late to go back now.*

Finally, I stepped into Fahada's large, rustic house. The whole family still bustled about the doorway in cheerful chaos as the older members prepared to leave.

The women turned their attention to greeting me.

"Fahada's in her room," Aunt Javaria whispered in my

ear as she hugged me. "She's feeling off and I think she needs a friend."

Upstairs, all was quiet, the noise of the family downstairs sounding blurry and distant.

With a hint of hesitation, I knocked on her door then paused for another moment before entering.

Fahada sat cross-legged on her bed, her posture erect and her gaze fixed on a point straight ahead.

"Are you…okay?" I asked.

Fahada barely twitched, but I caught the glint of a tear.

Internally I groaned.

"Are you still feeling depressed about the math test?"

"Have you been watching the news?" Fahada replied without blinking.

My brow furrowed.

"You know I used to live in Pakistan," Fahada started. "In the news, I saw the name of the town where my sisters live."

I knew Fahada adored her sisters. "You have three, right?"

"Yeah."

Unconscious of my movement, I stepped closer.

"ISIS invaded where they live, along with several other towns," she stated in a matter-of-fact way. "They stole crops from the outside farms—Hafsa and her husband own a farm. They captured all known Christians—like Izzati and her family."

My heart sank. "Oh, Fahada…"

"Part of the town was burnt to the ground. Many women and children were captured. Women were raped. I think of my sister Toshana—she was always the beautiful one."

Fahada caught her breath, and pressed her hands

against her temples.

I rubbed a hand over my face, trying to take it all in.

"Ari, help me!" Fahada cried. Too far away to fall into my arms, she latched her hands onto my shoulders instead.

I tensed and stared back at her with wide, startled eyes. My heart rate increased. I needed to calm this girl down.

"I don't know what to do, Ari!" She coughed and kept going, slightly short on breath. "I'm so confused. I don't know where to turn! I don't know what to do!" She sucked in a deep breath and burst into a hacking fit.

I forced myself to exhale and keep calm, but I could feel tightness spreading to each of my muscles as the intensity of the situation struck me. "Fahada, take a deep breath." I tried to keep my voice from shaking. "You can do it."

Fahada didn't bother to try. Her coughing fit continued, mixed with weeping. The coughs became smaller and smaller, yet more in number. Time froze as I watched helplessly. Panicked, I flew around her room, searching for her puffer. I found one and forced her fingers to curl around it. She shoved it in her mouth.

"Breathe!" I commanded. "Breathe!"

I willed Fahada to calm down.

Gradually her breathing returned to normal.

I shivered. Coughing and sneezing fits were common for my asthma-prone friend—anything from stress, to weather, to dust could trigger it—but the energy behind this attack was intense.

Something caught in my throat, and I fought against the gathering tears. "One day your asthma is going to kill you!" I shouted. "You need to keep that puffer on you at all times. Do you not even care, Fahada?" My own tears gushed down. "Don't you understand? You are the only real friend I have! I don't want you to die."

Fahada's head turned a notch toward me, and then one more, and then another until she was looking at me square in the face. Her swollen, lifeless stare bored into my head. Then, a little spark landed in her eyes, and her face twisted as if in pain. Words slid smoothly, even lifelessly, from her mouth.

"I care. I care very much. And I'm scared. I'm scared very much. I'm so afraid to die, very much afraid."

And, then, finally, she released her stare.

I swallowed. "I'll take care of your cousins."

Rapidly I changed course. Once I had started toward the door, I could hardly stop. Anything to get away from the terror and darkness weighing on her heart and permeating her room. But, I did stop. I turned back to my friend. Fahada was sliding a leather-bound book out of a messy stack.

I watched her movements. "You'll be okay?" My voice shook, and I paused to shove down my anxiety. "I won't leave if you want me to stay."

Fahada rested her forehead on the flat of her hand. "Don't worry about me."

Her words didn't help. Now that she had trusted me with her pain, I felt responsible for her. "Take care of yourself, okay? Read from that book you pulled out if it helps—or how about some painting? Just get yourself calmed down."

Fahada nodded almost imperceptibly, and immediately I turned and fled down the stairs.

I started to slow down near the kitchen. I practiced some deep breathing.

"I can't quite reach it!" A childish voice whined. My mind still whirled, but I could tell that something was up.

"Oh, Fahada," I whispered.

A sense of unease settled upon my spirit. But, I had to move on.

"Just get down, Alia! Ammi's going to get mad at us."

"But, I want it!"

Yay, another thing to deal with.

I tip-toed softly into the kitchen. A chair had been pulled up to the counter. Rawan stood wringing her eight-year-old hands on one side of the chair, and Bassim and Omar waited on the other. The little baby, Najiya, was nowhere to be seen. On top of the counter was piled three large phone books, and on top of the phone books stood Alia.

"Come on down." I pursed my lips, forming what I determined to be an 'I'm here and now you're in trouble' expression. I methodically tapped the floor with my foot, completing the image.

The kids froze.

"I-I-I told them not to do it!" Rawan burst out.

"Tell me, Rawan, what was Alia trying to get?"

Alia's face puckered, and she answered for her sister. "Some very sweet, very good M&Ms—Ammi said we could have them!"

"At bedtime," Rawan added.

"Good news for you all." I said. "I have chocolate in my bag. But, first, where's Najiya?"

"We put her on the couch."

I winced, envisioning her little helpless body flailing and rolling off the couch and landing on her head. Immediately, I started marching toward the living room. "My bag is by the door, the chocolate is in the front pocket."

Shrieks of delight erupted from the kids.

"Rawan's in charge!" I added over my shoulder.

I discovered Najiya peacefully sleeping at the edge of the couch. How ironic—a baby fast asleep while everyone else is drowning in chaos. Ever so gently I picked up the princess and cuddled her to myself. Najiya, the only calm being in the building.

As it turned out, this moment with Najiya happened to be the only quiet moment before I put the kids to sleep. But, eventually, that is exactly what I did.

*　　　　*　　　　*

"Like a diamond in the sky, twinkle, twinkle, little star, how I wonder what you are," I sang softly.

Inch by inch, I pulled the door toward myself.

"Ariela," Rawan called from her position snuggled next to Alia. "Stars aren't diamonds."

Alia's still form jerked. "Yes, they are!"

"No," Rawan explained solemnly. "They are balls of fire in the sky."

"This is not true!" Alia insisted. "Ariela said they are diamonds herself! Didn't you?"

Amused, I leaned against the door frame.

"Rawan and Alia, have either of you ever seen a star up close?"

"I saw one through a telescope once!" Alia's round eyes lit up.

For a brief moment I wondered if the sparkle shining therein was exactly like the one that had shone in my eyes years ago—the day Daddy brought me out to see the stars. The day he first called me his starlight. A corner of my mouth lifted slightly at the bitter-sweet memory.

"That's not quite the same, Alia. None of us have ever been close to a star, so none of us can say for sure."

"But—" Alia wasn't even close to sleepy.

"I do know two things, though. If you were both stars, you two would be the most beautiful of them all. And, you need to be quiet so you can fall asleep.

Baby Najiya's cries floated from the next room into theirs.

"Why should we be quiet when Najiya is never quiet?"

"Because you know better."

This time, I didn't bother with shutting the door carefully.

I grinned. *Now I can have the baby all to myself.*

Leaning against Najiya's crib, I gently readjusted the baby in my arms. She stuck her thumb in her mouth and drooled contentedly all over my new peasant blouse. I pried my phone out of my tight front pocket and dialed with one finger.

"Hi, this is Alexander."

"Hi, Al—"

"Sorry that you've missed me—please leave a message and I will call you back later."

Beep.

Najiya screeched, flailing her arms.

"Hey," I started my message in a soothing tone. "I guess I'm just wondering how you're doing. I miss you. You must have forgotten to call me when you arrived. Next time you have the chance, you know my number. Bye."

The message ended in a loud wail from the sweet baby in my arms.

Bouncing Najiya up and down, I tried to recollect the lullabies I used to hear. I sang every single one, pulling them from the deep recesses of my memory until Najiya's cries finally subsided with "Rock-a-by Baby". She snuggled in deeper. Her slobber warmed my neck but her adorable presence warmed my heart.

Movement caught my attention, and I sleepily raised my eyes without lifting my head. The door slid the rest of the way open and Fahada padded her way toward me, a canvas alive with color in hand.

"Need to switch?" Fahada spoke calmly, and I felt relieved.

"I think Najiya has finally found her happy spot, but you can stay. Feeling better?"

Fahada settled herself beside me. "Yeah. Been doing some deep thinking. And some painting." She held up the canvas so I could see.

I smiled, thankful that Fahada had followed my recommendation.

The painting was divided into two distinct sides by two opposing speech bubbles. In the left speech bubble, a blaring-red sun beat upon an empty wasteland. A vibrantly colored snake darted out from the shade of a lone cactus. Despair pervaded the scene, imposing a weighty sense of hopelessness.

My eyes sped to the next speech bubble. A majestic, wide-trunked oak spread out through its allotted side. I recognized two pairs of bluebirds, one pair of chickadees, and another of robins perched among the tree's branches. Each beak was opened wide as if full of song, and each bird was paying the utmost attention to its mate. A sun, mostly hidden by the luscious leaves, did not fail to cast its hue, causing a cheerful, hopeful brightness to emanate from the leaves themselves.

I mentally contrasted the light from either side's sun. Yes, there the main difference lay.

"What do you think?" Fahada asked.

"Very artistic. Does it have a meaning?"

She flipped to the other side. Fahada's calligraphy spread across the page filled it with simple elegance.

Fahada read out loud. "You will no longer be called Deserted, and your land will not be called Desolate." She paused her reading. "No longer, Ariela! No longer deserted, no longer abandoned!" She continued, "Instead, you will be called, 'My Delight is in Her'."

I blinked. *Is she being influenced by Lilac?*

"It's a promise," Fahada added. "The LORD, the God of the Bible, will take delight in me. That verse is found in Isaiah 62."

"Could I see the other side again?"

I took it all in for a second time, this time through opened eyes. The blaring sun of the desert shouted at me, calling me deserted, desolate, worthless, hopeless, abandoned, alone. Shivers rushed down my spine. I tore my gaze away and soaked in the brilliance of the second part. The sun, shining through the tree's thriving branches, audaciously declared, "I delight in you!"

Fahada took the chance to speak. "I've been deserted. My dad left me for the mines and Jawid has abandoned any real relationship with me. I know what pain feels like, the pain of being torn apart from your family, of not knowing if they're safe… or dead… or in pain."

"Oh, Fahada, I am really, truly sorry."

"Don't be," Fahada said, "because although I was deserted, now I am delighted in. By God—Jesus—the God of the Bible! I have found what Jawid has been so desperately searching for all these years." She tapped the dark side of her painting. "For all that seeking, Jawid's still here," she said, staring off into the distance. "If only I could be the one to release him."

I stared at her blankly, stunned by the profound depth

and confidence of her words. Could her fear, her angst, her pain really have vanished—just like that?

"It still hurts, and I'm really quite exhausted after all this turmoil and wrestling. But, I have peace."

"Does... does that mean that you're a Christian now?" I asked slowly.

"Yes, I think so."

"But... but don't you think it's a little fast to make such a decision?"

Fahada laughed a light, musical laugh. "No, not at all. And Ariela," she said, her eyes searching my face, "I am no longer afraid to die."

Chapter 7

Never Forget

I twitched impatiently against a school locker, waiting for Fahada. I raised myself to my tip-toes in an effort to see over a couple of particularly tall guys. One turned around and smiled at me. *Woodlynd.* I instantly broke the gaze and attempted to sift through the crowd with my eyes.

Not afraid to die? How could she talk like that, as if death were at her door? *Fahada is thinking too deeply. Yes, that's it. She needs to start just "living life" again—and return to being the cheerful person she used to be.*

I rolled my eyes at myself, resettling into a more comfortable position. *I guess I should start following my own advice and relax, have fun.*

I watched Woodlynd out of the corner of my eye. He stepped out from his group of friends.

"Ariela! Looking for someone?" He asked, a hint of a twinkle in his eyes.

"Oh, hi, Woodlynd." My heart thumped. "Yeah, I'm just looking for Fahada."

"The one you always hang out with?"

"Yep."

"With her around, I can hardly find a chance to talk with you!" He teased.

Startled, I made the mistake of looking up. Our eyes locked for a moment.

"If she doesn't end up coming today, maybe we could sit together during lunch?" Woodlynd raised an eyebrow, as he always used to when indicating a question.

I nodded. "And catch up on each other's lives. I would like that!"

Someone tapped Woodlynd on the shoulder.

Woodlynd smiled apologetically at me. "Gotta go. See you!"

As I watched him leave, a smirk briefly crossed my face. I wish Jade could've heard this conversation.

With the taste of victory in my mouth, I found it less of a bug when Jade sat next to me in Pre-Cal. Fahada, of course, would have been much more ideal.

Even so—

"Bye, Jade!" I called as I swept past her, out of the stuffy room. *Spare time! And time to get some fresh air.* I marched right out of the school, around the back, until I finally reached the little garden in a corner.

For the first two months of high school—before I befriended Fahada—this had been my place of retreat. The chipper chirping of the songbirds, the random bursts of muffled, childish laughter from the other side of the building, and the bright flowers and stable oaks—it all mingled together to create a place of perfect refuge. When Fahada had come, she had joined me. Then it had become a place of laughter.

I glanced around to take in the colorful flowers. Instead, a wearied face stared back at me. It was Fahada, elbows resting on her knees as she sat on the single bench.

I stopped in my tracks. Inside I jumped.

Fahada smiled softly at me. A hint of red encircled her

eyes. "I knew you'd find me here."

Guess this ruins my lunch plans.

Blushing, I silently rebuked myself.

I slid next to her on the cold metal bench.

She flipped over a paper or a card that had been laying on her lap, and placed her puffer on top.

"Did you sleep through your alarm?"

"Big time." Fahada smiled wryly, angling her face toward me. Somehow, she looked years older than she was.

"Did you cut yourself?" A thin jagged line ran down an inch of her cheek.

"Jawid threw a glass."

I gasped. "At you?"

"No, no! At the wall. When I told him what happened."

"That you became a Christian? He wouldn't be that upset, would he?" Already concern was sweeping across my face.

"It was a combination of everything, I think. I actually didn't straight out tell him I accepted Jesus—just that I wanted to go to church with a friend. You know her— Lilac. Anyway, Jawid was pretty quiet at first. I knew we were both thinking about Izzati—our sister who became a Christian. He picked up a glass of water to drink—and then I told him what had happened at home, our old home. You know, the attack. He threw the glass at the wall and a shard bounced back, cutting my skin. Then Jawid yelled, 'Where is God in all of this?'"

Fahada's eyes drifted shut. "And I was up late, too. I'm pretty tired."

My head reeled. I didn't understand how Fahada could just be so casually matter-of-fact about this. This was no small deal!

Light laughter and quiet voices drifted into range. I stilled, scanning for any intruders.

Fahada kept speaking. "I phoned up Lilac. Some verses she prayed over me—"

Whatever she said next faded out as a gently swinging hand appeared. Finally, the owners of the voices in question appeared around the corner—a boy and a girl. The girl's distinct, carefully styled make-up caught my attention—Jade. She pretended not to see me. I willed her tall, sandy haired partner to turn around and look toward me, but his face was turned toward Jade.

"I have to be on time for lunch," he was saying.

Could it be? No—it couldn't. At least they aren't holding hands.

Soon they passed our alcove and I returned my attention to my friend.

"That's from Psalm 42. Beautiful, isn't it?" Fahada's tone held a hint of thoughtful reflection. "So, I did, Ari. I did. I put my hope in God. But I'm discouraged about Jawid. I want to tell him about my relationship with Jesus—like, actually tell him. But, I'm concerned for him. He used to be such a sweet brother... but he's different now. He needs Jesus, too."

"Oh, come on, Fahada. Don't you see?" I kept my tone patient. "Being concerned for him won't help a thing. You're not responsible for him, you're responsible for yourself. You need to do what's best for you and leave it at that. Don't do anything too risky!"

"But, I have to tell him that I've accepted Jesus. He has a right to know."

"Okay," I tried again. "Maybe you should, but wait a bit until he's calmed down more to tell him about your new faith."

"No, I can't. I won't."

"Fahada, please! For my sake! I'm worried about you. Wait at least a couple days, think about it." I took her chilly hands in mine, silently pleading with her.

She hesitated. "If that's what you want."

"Good. Now we should go inside to eat lunch."

Without Woodlynd, I added silently, begrudgingly. And I thought again about Jade's tall companion with sandy hair.

The walk inside remained unearthly silent, both our hearts engaged in internal battles.

I straightened up at the sight of a crowd inside the school doors; somehow, I felt smaller. A crowd was the one thing that could choke out my thoughts.

Fahada's expression visibly changed. She was back in her prime. I prepared myself for a sudden burst of energy or exclamation.

Instead, she turned to me and, for a brief moment, rested her hand on my back. "Ariela, what's on your mind? I feel like something is bugging you—more than we already talked about."

Fahada wasn't going to beat around the bush.

"I just need a friend, Fahada. I just need a friend."

Fahada placed an arm fully around my shoulders. "We're very much alike. Have you ever realized that?"

I shook my head slightly. "No. What makes you think that?"

The crowd tightened around us, and Fahada let go of my shoulders. She spoke louder to be heard clearly above the others. "Lilac explained in our phone call yesterday. Both of us feel like we have lost our dads and both of us feel like we've lost our brothers. I think I know how you feel now, too."

I'm sure a question mark was floating across my face as I looked at my friend. "Maybe I should give that Lilac a call."

"You should! She'd be super pleased!" Fahada skipped slightly.

"What did you learn?"

Fahada paused her steps.

I noticed a distinct shine to her face, a strong hope and confidence emanating from her countenance.

Fahada's burning eyes latched on mine. "Ariela, never forget that Jesus is worth it. Always."

My jaw tensed, and I wished I had a piece of gum to gnaw on. "You're going to tell your brother tonight. Aren't you?"

"I'm going to leave the keys to my locker inside of yours. I have a shoe box in there, and the picture I showed you the other day."

"You're hiding them from Jawid?"

"Yeah."

A young teacher scurried into a classroom nearby, throwing me a quick wave as she passed. I smiled back briefly.

"But you won't have anything to hide after tonight, will you?" I scanned Fahada's face, searching for further clues as to what she was thinking and feeling.

Fahada shook her head. "That's not the point. I don't know how Jawid will react. He may blame my decision on the 'bad influences' of school. He's already been seriously considering homeschooling me."

"Okay," I said, nodding slowly. "So, you want me to bring them to you if you don't come back?"

"No. The treasures I have in that shoe box, and that picture—they would be yours then."

I just shook my head. "This is all happening so fast, Fahada, I'm not sure what to think."

We now stood by the door to my classroom which was rapidly filling with students.

Fahada flung her arms around me. "Don't worry, you'll always be my best friend!"

A lump formed in my throat and I swallowed.

"Well, I'm proud of you for taking that stand. Don't forget to call me after you have the conversation." I faked a smile. "I'll just be dying of curiosity!"

Fahada squeezed my shoulder. "Of course, you're concerned for me." Fahada flashed me a trademark grin. "Never forget—Jesus is worth it, always."

Chapter 8

Dreadful Silence

With trembling fingers, I tapped the numbers for Fahada's cell number. I double-checked the small numbers at the top of the screen. 9:21 PM. *Why is Fahada taking so long?* I took a deep breath, trying to calm my anxiety. I didn't understand my fear. Fahada must have just forgotten to call me. *She just forgot. Fahada always forgets things.*

One ring. I waited. Two rings. Three rings. Four rings. Five rings.

I started to pace.

Six rings. And then it stopped.

Nothing. I just wanted to hear her voice!

"Hello?" I said hesitantly.

A raspy, unintelligible sound greeted my ears.

Must be a bad connection or something.

"Hello?" I repeated, more forcefully this time.

Another quiet, raspy sound reached my ears. "Aaaa. Eeee."

Is that breathing?

"Fahada, are you okay?"

"A-a-a-ah"

Is she choking?

"Speak to me, girl!"

"Fahada, open up!" Someone with a muffled, male voice said. "Fahada! We can talk this through. I won't hurt you, I promise."

My mind raced, desperately searching for the missing piece in this confusing puzzle.

Thump. Thump. Thump.

Silence.

I resumed pacing.

A drawn-out creak of a door.

The masculine voice came out clearer now, but quieter, more heavy-hearted. "Oh, no. Fahada, I'm so sorry."

Straining to hear, I picked up movement. I perceived some rustling, a groan, another creak, and then again that silence—that dreadful silence. The depth of that lack of noise echoed inside my body, bouncing from one rib cage to the other: an endless sound of emptiness.

I tried to connect the dots of what was happening, but it felt like drawing lines in between the stars, trying to find constellations. It was like being lost in a maze, a maze I had never wanted to step into anyway.

Yet, there was one thing I knew for a fact: Fahada did attempt to tell her brother about her conversion. The foolish girl with such a foolish friend. I shut my eyes, the scene filling my sight with colorful darkness. I saw her pivoting back and forth as Jawid shook her shoulders. I saw her falling to the floor as Jawid stormed out of the room. I saw her weeping uncontrollably, the sobs stealing the room her breath used to fill.

No, no! I can't do it. This isn't happening—this didn't happen. Fahada is okay.

Guilt berated me tauntingly. It shoved a malicious finger into my face, accusing me of the deliberate lie.

And who could I turn to?

Then it occurred to me. *Lilac. I must talk with Lilac.*

Panic transformed my fingers into clumsy sticks as my fumbling fingers dialed her number.

The emotionless, high-pitched ring grated my already shredded nerves. It wasn't even that it was emotionless—it was that it was eternally consistent, never changing tone, never skipping a beat.

Please God, if you're real then you know I need this!

I was about to hang up—or throw the phone against a wall.

Abruptly the ringing halted. I bent over as if attacked by a gripping cramp. I longed for the consistent irritation of the ring tone once more. The immediate void crippled me.

"Hello? Lilac speaking." The distance between "hello" and "Lilac" was all it took from her voice sounding distracted and far gone to light and professional. Of course, then, the latter were facades.

I wouldn't take too much of her time.

"Lilac," I emphasized through gritted teeth. "Explain to me what you told Fahada yesterday. This is no time for pleasantries, I'm sorry."

Instantly I felt guilty for my harsh tone.

"I just gave her some Scripture references—"

I plastered a smile on my face, hoping it would help soften my tone. "Where are they found? I'll grab my Bible on my bed-stand."

Of course, it was her Bible. But I only thought of it midway through.

"Romans 5:10. It's in the New Testament, sixth book. Should be highlighted."

For a moment my search was quiet.

"Read it aloud when you get there, okay?"

"Romans 5:10: 'For if, while we were enemies, we were reconciled to God through the death of His Son, then how much more, having been reconciled, will we be saved by His life!'"

I latched onto the last phrase. "'We will be saved through His life,'" I repeated cynically. "That must have been what gave her the confidence to risk it."

"No, actually, it was the part that said, 'While we were enemies, we were reconciled to God through the death of His Son.'"

"What does God have against Fahada?" I asked irritably.

Lilac began slowly, "Ariela—"

I bit my tongue, but I released it too soon.

"The 'Lord'," I stressed, "in my mind, acts in a way reminiscent to communist dictators." I steeled my grip on the phone, not caring if I crushed it. "He rips from my desperate grasp the comparatively little I claim as my own and distributes it evenly among all people, taking only the best for himself. It's time for a rebellion, and today I will launch it."

Lilac was silent.

I covered my face in my hands. What kind of raving lunatic was I? Ah, some claim the combination of being a deep thinker and feeler at the same time is painful. Personally, I was surprised my own intensity hadn't caused any explosions as of yet. Any explosions right near my head.

Only Lilac's breathing told me she was still there.

It wasn't so bad to experience mere internal intensity. It was the impulsive outbursts that shamed me.

"Ariela? Could I pray for you?"

I kicked my mind back into gear, hoping there would

be enough emotional fuel to push me through the conversation.

For a moment I considered. Maybe I needed all the help I could get.

And I thought back to the raspy choking which greeted my ears just minutes before. The gags that begged for air, yet came up empty. I shivered. And I remembered why I was angry and what I had come to find out.

"Ariela, maybe God deserves to be given a chance."

"I just want to know if Fahada's going to be okay! Lilac, that's really all it is! This God who claims we're His enemies—can I trust Him that He'll save His own?"

"Those who know Him will trust Him. He does not abandon anyone who comes to Him. For Fahada, for you—if you come to Him for help, He won't abandon you."

I could hear myself above the roar of my heart again. "Thank you, Lilac. That's all I wanted to know."

I hung up even as my cell vibrated, tickling my palm.

I checked it absently.

I read over the message once, going so far as to carelessly depress the circular button at the bottom. Instantly, the words were gone. For a moment I remained paralyzed. I hadn't just read those words, had I?

It was a forwarded message from Uncle Dallas— originally from Fahada's uncle—and it included the wish of a dying friend.

Uncle Dallas told me that although he was currently stuck in traffic, he'd be home soon to take me to the hospital. The words flew over my head.

The second car is still here.

The events that came next blurred together in my mind... zipping across the house looking for my purse, speeding along the highway, oblivious to the fact that I only had my learners permit, and rushing through the hospital doors. I remember the lady at the desk mumbling something about Room 3, with her brother and his visitors in Room 4. Then I was scurrying through the hallways, searching for the door number. Moments later, I stood beside the bed where Fahada lay motionless.

Fahada.

My eyesight blurred and my breath came out in huge gasps. A silver machine fed her air through a tube. A small rectangular box with wires that traveled beneath her t-shirt monitored the rate of her heart in numbers. An electrocardiogram revealed the rate as a graph. What shocked me most was the bandages on her face.

A male nurse in a traditional green suit stood nearby.

I knelt by her bed. "Fahada. Oh, Fahada. What happened?"

The nurse answered me. "Car crash—it was a double roll-over. She took on a lot of physical damage and her oxygen levels are extremely low. We're still analyzing the situation."

I swished saliva around in my mouth to relieve the dryness and swallowed. "She has asthma." I bit down on my lip but released before a canine tooth punctured flesh. "I think her brother was trying to take her to the hospital after a severe attack."

I reached to touch Fahada's hand. Tears streaked down my face. Was I about to lose my friend?

Bubble gum ice cream.

Sparkly hijabs.

Mischievous smiles.

"Jesus is worth it. Always."

It was the bubble gum ice cream that broke me.

"Fahada?" I voiced tentatively.

Seconds morphed into eternity as I waited with bated breath for a voice I never heard.

Instead a gloved hand settled on my shoulder. It was the nurse again, asking me to leave.

So soon? I forced myself to refocus and to analyze the situation. I studied the electrocardiogram, but something was wrong. The line was straight. Fahada's heart was dead.

Something in me collapsed. I didn't know what it was.

A part of redistribution, I knew. *And the Instigator only takes the best for Himself.* The thought served as little comfort to me.

Chapter 9

Hidden in a Vulnerable Place

Crossing my arms, I briskly walked out of the hospital room. A group of three nurses who were clustered just outside of the next door whispered with barely audible voices, but the sharp note of the "sss" sound grated against my ears. I continued down the eternal hallway, an endless sea of dull grey.

I turned a corner and the lady at the counter smiled at me with a sugary smile, drawing my attention to her bright red, off-centered lipstick.

Both sets of doors beeped when I opened them.

As I stepped out into the cool evening, I squinted my eyes to adjust to the lighting. The potlights along the hospital's overhang revealed a tiny ant emerging from a crack in the sidewalk. I lifted my foot and intentionally lowered it down, taking pleasure as I squished the ant underneath my heel. How I wished I could end Jawid's piddly life just as easily as the ant's. I knew it was his fault.

My hands loosely retained a hold on the steering wheel. I was in the left lane, but cars from the right passed me. Soon the spotless, large, white doors, so familiar by now, loomed ahead of me. I considered allowing the speed of the vehicle to carry me into the doors and out the window of the vehicle. But my speed was too slow and my seatbelt was buckled. I parked and stumbled inside, escaping numbly—slowly— to my bedroom.

I couldn't rest. I couldn't think.

How it got there, I didn't know. But, when a knock resounded on my bedroom door, I was staring blankly at the open Bible on my lap.

Uncle Dallas, dad, walked in.

"Having a hard time concentrating?" He lowered himself onto his knees beside my bed.

"Yeah."

"I can tell—your Bible is upside down."

"Ari—" dad's voice cracked and he didn't say more. His breathing was shaky. My big, big daddy was crying. For me. His tears dripped onto the Bible's pages. I watched them fall.

And then I considered my real daddy; the night he had left me; the tears wetting my hair.

"I know."

Uncle Dallas didn't seem to hear me. "I'm sorry that you caught my text while you were away. I don't know if you're aware, but—" Uncle Dallas inhaled and let out a long sigh. "Fahada is dead. It looks like she had a severe asthma attack that went unattended. The car crash did her in. I'm sorry."

"Her brother, Jawid, just has minor injuries."

I could feel my face getting warmer and warmer with anger. "Thanks, Dad—Uncle Dallas, I mean. I'd like to be by myself now." It took every bit of my strength to say those simple words calmly.

I flipped Lilac's Bible right-side-up.

He stood up. "Ari, it's eleven o'clock. You should be going to bed soon."

I wasn't ready. By the time the door closed, I was nearly vibrating with angry emotion.

I glared at the Bible. Picking it up in my shaking hands, it felt heavy, lifeless.

"Ahh! I just can't do this!" I screamed, not caring if he heard. The Bible left my hand and flew through the air, smacking the wall with an empty thud.

Immediately, I leaped off my bed and snatched it up again. I wrapped my fingers around a handful of pages and yanked viciously, the pages ripping out with a sickening tear. Soon the Bible was merely a pile of torn and crumpled sheets of paper.

"God," I spoke His name as if it were disgusting. The sense of betrayal overwhelming my mind pressed a dark stain upon my heart. "I came this close, this close to giving in to You. Why does 'this close' always have to be too much? God! You're too much for me. I trusted that You would keep her safe. I surmised that You, at the very least, could do it better than me." My own words of vulnerability stabbed at me. I paused a few heartbeats. The heat of rage flowed over my defenseless soul.

"I trusted Alexander to give me joy. Let me ask You: who called him away? You. When he failed, I trusted Fahada to keep me lighthearted. I'll ask You again: who weighted her down? You did. Then I trusted in You to keep her safe. One more question: who tore her away? Who broke her? You were the One. What an utter fool—I repeat! What an utter fool I was to believe in You!"

Breathing hard, I said nothing more. I couldn't.

Carefully I picked up each and every shredded page of the Bible and tossed them in the garbage can.

"So much for loving me. I'm done."

I crawled over my bed toward the window seat and

peered out the window, searching for something—I didn't know what. The October night was already closing in, and stars were starting to light up the sky. Yet the light inside of me was quickly fading. I wasn't the starlight my daddy used to tell me I was. And now, when I needed him most, my daddy wasn't here to wipe the tears from my eyes. He wasn't here to cuddle me and tell me that it would all be okay.

The brightness of the stars irritated me. I swiped the curtains closed. I had to hide. I fumbled my way around the now-dark room until my fingers found the curtain from my closet. I shoved shoes out of the way and hunched down inside beneath the hanging skirts and dresses. Then I pulled the closet curtain shut. Maybe here I would be safe.

I sat there in silence. The steady tick-tock of the grandfather clock in the next room floated into my hearing range.

"My friend, Fahada. She was my friend." I wrapped my arms around myself and numbly rocked back and forth, back and forth.

Tick, tock. Tick, tock. Tick, tock. The sound reverberated inside my head. A dull sound. An echoing sound. A sound that I could not escape.

Is this what prison's like?

After several moments, a realization hit me. I rubbed the bottom of the curtain between my thumb and first finger. This was where Alexander had hidden that night long ago. I relived that moment in my imagination: remembering my intense fear, my relieved anger. My fear had cheated me, I had indeed been safe.

"But, I wasn't; I'm not. Alexander left me, too," I said.

Snippets of painful memories flooded my mind. They

swept me away into the deep recesses of my memory, I found myself floundering in that place of unending torment.

A million voices swarmed my head with tumultuous noise.

I groaned, stuffing my fingers into my ears in a useless attempt to end the racket.

A pleasant face began to take shape before my eyes.

My back arched and I cried, "Daddy! Don't leave me! Don't go! Daddy!"

His image faded, and Alexander took its place. His mouth opened as if to speak, as if to call me, then; instead, his image contorted and a disgusted smile stretched across his face. I reached out, but he wasn't there. Only darkness was there.

Then I heard it, loud and clear, in the familiar tone of my lost friend, "*Ariela*".

"Fahada! Where are you? Fahada!" I started to my feet, then collapsed back to the floor.

How stupid could I be? No one was speaking to me. I wrapped my arms around myself again, urgently trying to warm up my shivering shell. The voices continued.

Chapter 10

First Time For Everything

I moaned and forced my heavy eyelids to open. I crawled out of the closet, my newly appointed bed for almost a week, and pushed on my knees for leverage to stand. My head throbbed and my back ached. Then a fact hit me with the force of a train engine—It was Monday morning.

I limped down the stairs and forced myself to ignore my stomach's protests. Briefly I considered grabbing a banana before school but decided against it. As I opened the door the chilly wind hit my face like a slap. I lowered myself down to the top step to rest, not even having the energy to shiver.

Numbly I lifted myself up and kept moving. I reached the bus stop, ignoring the curious stares of my classmates and strangers.

"Hey, if you want you can borrow my jacket. I have a sweater underneath anyway. It's pretty cold." I didn't recognize the feminine voice. I didn't look up to check its owner.

I tried to blink. It felt like trying to smile with dry lips that stuck together. The voice didn't sound like Fahada's. Where was she? The gears inside my head gradually began to turn. Fahada was dead. Spikes sprung from the mental gears, effortlessly tearing and slicing through my brain.

The internal agony crippled me with a silent grip, somehow deeper than the night before. It settled into the pit of my stomach and stayed.

Fahada is gone. Forever.

The bus arrived and picked us up. Like a robot, I found and sat down in my normal spot. A short, chubby boy with wide-rimmed glasses hesitated at my row. In response, I set my backpack on the seat beside me. *Not on my first school day without Fahada.*

I slid my iPhone out of my pocket and stared at it blankly until it woke up. *Three missed calls* read a pop-up. Checking the call display, I discovered that two were from Alexander and one from Lilac.

"I'll worry about this later," I mumbled, leaning my head back against the seat.

At noon I picked a table in the corner of the cafeteria to sit at. I let my head drop to the table and felt myself begin to doze off.

The lights grew brighter in my eyes. The pain in my gut crystallized. My nose twitched, receiving a new scent in its nostrils. My stomach rumbled, and I remembered I hadn't packed a lunch.

"Oh, you're awake," a masculine voice greeted my ears.

I shifted slightly and willed myself to look up, coming face-to-face with emerald eyes.

"Hey," Woodlynd said. "Care for some company?"

I focused in on a few crumbs scattered across the table.

"I brought you some food—garlic sausage soup and Italian bread." He pulled out a chair beside me and sat down.

"Okay," a voice too hoarse to be mine answered weakly.

I stuck the spoon in the soup and began to devour the

meal, not bothering to look up.

"Are you thinking about Fahada?" Woodlynd asked.

I rolled my shoulders in an effort to relieve their tension.

Woodlynd stood up and came behind me. His strong hands began to knead my sore muscles.

I didn't want to be touched. I didn't want anyone near me.

"Just relax," Woodlynd said. "I want to help."

"Fahada's dead."

Woodlynd's hands paused their work. "I heard on the loud speakers, and I thought that I had to check up on you."

A slight moan escaped my lips.

He resumed rubbing my shoulders. "I hardly know what to say." He paused again, obviously still trying to wrap his mind around it. "What happened?"

"Not now," I said. "I'm too tired to talk."

Woodlynd spoke slower now, keeping his tone calm and strong for my sake. "That's alright. This must be really hard for you. If you ever need someone to talk to, I'm here. I'll write down my cell number for you in a minute. And maybe we could sit together at lunch sometimes?"

I shrugged. "If… if that's what you want." Drawing in a large, deep breath, I forced my mind to contemplate the idea. "Honestly," I whispered then tried to utter the words 'I don't care' but they refused to flip off my tongue. "I would like that."

*   *   *

I stepped through our doorway and dropped my already half-off backpack onto the floor.

"Hey," Dad greeted, pushing himself off his recliner.

I frowned at the sight; the recliner was facing backward

in order to provide full view of the front door.

"I didn't want to miss you accidentally," Dad said sheepishly.

"You're so sweet," I said dryly.

He gave me a hug. "So, Love, did you make any new friends?"

I squirmed out of his arms. I shot him one scathing glance, then marched up the stairs.

"New friends," I muttered. "New friends? Does he think I could replace Fahada just like that?" A tear streaked down my face and I swiped at it with irritation. Mom appeared at the top of the stairs.

"It's okay to mourn," she said.

I didn't even bother meeting her eyes. "You picked a good time to start caring."

I turned sideways to squeeze past her and disappeared into my room.

Laying on my bed, my wearied mind drifted in and out of sleep. Dreams and daydreaming merged into one drawn out saga. Woodlynd's offer to sit with me at lunch turned into a proposal to be my date at the prom, and his willingness to walk me home from school merged into dreams of moonlit walks. Sparkles, rings, flowers, special winks, private jokes, and first kisses permeated my thoughts and covered the ache inside. As the clock struck eleven, I rolled over and cried.

Chapter 11

Woodlynd and I

Sunday, November 27th

Woodlynd handed me his mittens and crouched down. I slipped his mittens over mine to provide extra protection from the winter temperature.

Woodlynd quietly moved off the overgrown biking trail and toward a squirrel. He drew one step closer to the evergreen tree, ducking to avoid its protruding branches. In slow motion his hands reached out until they appeared to meet the creature's deep brown fur.

A slight smile froze on my face as I watched with bated breath.

The squirrel's head shot up in alarm. Its tiny feet propelled the creature forward—but it was too late. One of Woodlynd's hands had already clenched its tail while the other he quickly wedged underneath its belly.

"Ow!" Woodlynd yelped, instantly withdrawing his hand. The squirrel darted out and vanished up the tree, chattering furiously all the way.

I tried not to giggle, the mood broken. "You okay there?"

"Just a scratch," he said. "It shouldn't have stopped me."

"At least you didn't hurt the little guy!" I knelt beside

Woodlynd under the tree. My jeans instantly soaked up the light dusting of snow. Many layers above me, I briefly caught a glimpse of our friend's bushy tail.

"He left his snack behind. Here, Ariela, keep it as a souvenir." Woodlynd pressed an acorn into the palm of my hand.

"You're so silly, Woodlynd." Playfully I stuck my tongue out at him.

His gaze met mine and lingered for a moment.

I smiled, leaning back against the tree's rough trunk. Woodlynd joined me, as I had hoped.

The squirrel forgotten, I let out a contented breath. I laid my head on Woodlynd's shoulder and snuggled close for warmth. And, well, just because I wanted to be close. "Woodlynd, I don't know how I would have come through these last few weeks without you. I just love you so much."

In response Woodlynd rested his head on top of mine. I smiled bigger.

"How long has it been since Fahada died?" Woodlynd asked after a moment's pause.

"Almost five weeks now," I said. The words slid out naturally. Fahada's death was already becoming the measuring stick of my life: "This happened three months before Fahada died", or "that was five days after". Much had changed. After Fahada's funeral, I had dropped all contact with the family. There was an unspoken awkwardness that no one wanted to cross, highlighted by my brewing anger against Jawid. And then there was my new relationship with Woodlynd—this was my light. I sighed. My parents still didn't approve of our relationship. Even today, I let them assume I was hanging out with a new friend named Tiffany. In reality, I had only chatted with Tiffany a few times at school, and nothing more. Fahada's death was still too fresh to let any female friend take her spot.

I bit my lip softly. "There's just so many things I don't know, Woodlynd. On the night Fahada died... the night she told Jawid about her relationship with Jesus... did Jawid blaze out at her? Or hurt her? Was the stress of Jawid's response what caused her asthma attack? Or was it more accidental? I mean, I don't know Jawid at all. Maybe I'm too quick in pointing fingers. After all, he did attempt to drive her to the hospital. But as we both know, that didn't work out too well." I straightened up, lifting my head from Woodlynd's shoulder. "And then there's the matter of God. Remember when I told you what she said, that 'Jesus is worth it always?' Is Jesus worth Fahada's death? Or is God even alive?" I returned my head to Woodlynd's shoulder. "I just don't know."

Woodlynd rubbed circles on my knee, reminding me that I hadn't returned his mittens. In an instant they were off and on his lap.

Woodlynd didn't seem to notice as he focused on presenting me with a well thought out reply. He let out a puff of air, forming a foggy-white cloud. "I want you to be careful with this God thing, Ariela. Many people get sucked into it in the hard times of life, when they're most vulnerable. My mom, for example. But you have me to stand next to you, and I don't want you to get hurt by a God who steals life early. If you accepted Jesus, it would vastly change our relationship."

"I won't," I spoke up quickly, before he could say anything further. "You're enough for me." I quickly shot a glance toward his eyes. Despite the warning tone of his words, the eyes below his knitted brows were warm with concern. What a wonderful boyfriend I had found, one who treasured me so; I relaxed.

"Good," he said, like the matter was closed.

Woodlynd pulled on the mittens which had previously gone unnoticed. He stood up and offered me his hand, which I took. His large hand enveloped my small one. As we walked, neither of us let go. I felt comfortably locked in that spot next to Woodlynd, as if I finally had found my place in the world, and my home.

Hands gently swinging, Woodlynd and I emerged from the trees and onto the gravel road near our school. Hesitantly and subtly, a lilting song breached the crusty soil of my heart. A song that, if it were a jewel, would be an emerald. A song that, if it were a time, would be always. A song that, if it were a person, would be us—Woodlynd and me.

As we passed by the first couple houses on my street, I caught a glimmer of movement from the corner of my eye. I was sure it wasn't a flickering Christmas light, though colorful strings of lights bordered many roofs. Glancing around nervously, I decided to be safe and slipped my hand out of Woodlynd's. Peering up into the window of our neighbors' house, I caught the stare of newly married Sarah Whitney. She smiled knowingly, but didn't stop watching. I picked up my pace, not slowing down until her house disappeared from sight.

I halted right before our driveway and threw my arms around Woodlynd for a quick hug. "See you tomorrow?"

"Of course." Woodlynd kept me in his arms a moment longer. "Shall we go for ice cream?"

I pulled back and cupped my cold cheeks with my mittens. Woodlynd was, of course, referring to the place where Lilac worked. My relationship with Lilac was another thing that Fahada's death had changed. Ever since that point I had distanced myself from her. Yes, partially because her reassurances about Fahada had not come true. God had abandoned Fahada, even though she came to Him. Yet still, I didn't fully blame Lilac. She was just ignorant. What I really feared were the caring eyes and gentle insistence to hear my heart and how I was really doing. That is why I hadn't gone to the ice cream shop or answered any of her texts for the last several weeks. I made a face. Maybe it wasn't right to leave her in suspense.

Finally, I answered. "I feel like ice cream is more of a summer treat."

Woodlynd shrugged. "At least it would be inside and out of the cold."

I laughed. "That is true! Talking of being out of the cold, I should probably head in now. We can text back and forth this evening."

"Sure, all good."

I blew him a kiss and dashed inside, suddenly longing for the warmth of a fire and a cup of hot chocolate.

Chapter 12

The Hurt and the Healer

As I slammed the front door behind me moments later, Mom looked up, tossing a shock of straightened brown hair to the side. Her new haircut looked sharp.

Mom spoke into the home phone by her ear. "Ariela's here. Do you want to speak with her?"

Mom handed the phone to me. "It's Alexander."

I stabilized the phone between my ear and shoulder to free my hands while I removed my mittens and coat.

"Hey, Alexander. How're you?"

"Great! I've been super busy. Friday was the youth Christmas party. And just this morning I was preaching, which sure required a lot of thinking and prep time."

I found myself grinning. Alexander did tend to get straight to the point, enthusiasm always included. "Hey, I told you that thinking was a useful exercise to practice. Good job!"

Alexander chuckled. "Yeah, all that thinking has been pretty stretching. Get it? Exercise, stretching?"

Smirking, I settled onto a couch and pulled a fuzzy blanket around me. "I'm sure. But no worries there. It takes time to learn new things."

From the adjacent couch Mother mumbled something

under her breath. I looked up to see her lips uncharacteristically turned up at the corners. My grin widened.

"Anyway, that's my week," Alexander said. "What's new for you this November, Ari?"

I wiggled my cold toes. "Nothing much. I got started on my Christmas shopping…"

"Oh, yeah! And now that you have your driver's license you can drive yourself," Alexander said.

I nodded. "Which is nice. Plus, there's babysitting and hanging out with friends—all normal stuff, really."

"That's right, you were visiting with Tiffany today?"

I froze, all of a sudden incredibly conscious of Mom's listening ears. "That's right," I said. "We went for a walk."

"Sounds like the kind of thing you and Fahada would do together. In my head, I kind of imagined that you would want any new friendships to look a little different."

I mulled on that one for a moment, not wanting to trip on my tongue and expose my lie.

"Or maybe you've moved on faster than I expected?" Alexander waited to see if I would reply. I didn't. "I don't think that's how it is, though."

I mumbled quickly, "Well, it's just a typical girl thing to go on a walk."

"Sure," Alexander said. "Still, it reminds me. I was thinking about this earlier today, and I was reminded of Mary—you know, the mother of Jesus. She endured social rejection because of Jesus during her pregnancy, and then when He died, her heart was pierced through on His behalf."

My eyes wandered the room as I tried to grasp where Alexander was going with this. His tone was solemn now, and it made me uncomfortable.

Alexander continued, "Yet she put her hope in God. In fact, she was honored that she could play such a special part in God's great plan. Her heart of submission is a major part of what makes her so well known and loved to this day. And, Ari, it could be the same for you."

I blinked hard and straightened up, as if a spring had suddenly been released. "What are you trying to say, Alexander? That I'm not handling this Fahada deal well?"

From her position on the next couch, Mom turned her head to watch.

I started walking up the stairs while Alexander hurried to explain himself. "No, no, Ari, that's not what I'm trying to say—at all!"

I scurried up the rest of the steps to my bedroom and leaned up against the door. My head spun. I couldn't place a finger on why this was such a sore spot. I wasn't even in a bad mood! Why did this sting so much?

I took a deep breath. I let it out too soon. "Then what are you saying, Alex? You're trying to fix me, right? You can't fix anything and everything, you know." I shut my eyes.

"That's not what I'm trying to say." Alexander trailed off.

I sighed, struggling to maintain a calm tone. Despite myself, my voice cracked. "Why don't you trust me? I'm not just your little sister anymore! I'm growing up, you know."

"Hey, all I'm trying to say is…" Alexander paused to take a deep breath. "I'm sorry, Ari. I picked a bad time to bring this up."

I worked my lip. Alexander was right. I wasn't as healed, as I was pretending to be. I waited for Alexander to tack on the 'I told you so' comment.

He didn't.

"Alexander, I just—I mean, I don't know why..."

"That's okay, Ariela, I understand."

"No, that's just it, Alexander!" I exclaimed. "You don't understand."

Alexander interrupted me again. "I do, though! You feel like you're always being treated like a little kid when in reality all you need is a little support."

"No." I felt relieved by my calmer, informative tone. "It's like this: I can't put my hope in God like Mary did." I gave Alexander a moment to process. "I just cannot place my 'hope' in a God who takes life early. That sure shows how much He values us."

"No," Alexander said in shock. "No," he said a little louder. "And if you think of it, Ari, it was the same way with Mary and Jesus. Jesus died when he was just 33 years old! Just think how Mary's heart would have felt as Jesus' mother."

"Just think about how my friend's heart did feel, and does feel," I rebutted. I desperately wanted to make Alexander understand. I strained my words, willing him to catch my drift. I wasn't angry anymore; I just needed to know I was right and understood. "Listen to yourself, Alex! You made my point for me. God took life early. When He did, it hurt people—badly! Do you see what I mean? A 33-year-old son? Dead. A 16-year-old friend? Dead. Why? To me it defies all logic."

I settled into a more comfortable position, now sure that my reasoning had passed the test.

"You're right, Ari, it does defy all logic. Just not as you think." Alexander cleared his throat to signal a change in topic.

I broke in hastily. "That's it? No rebuttal? No nothing?

I thought you'd have something more to say."

"I do, but I'm not going to say it unless you ask."

I rolled my eyes. What right did Alexander think he had to play a game like this with me?

This was why I liked Woodlynd—he, at least, answered my questions directly and with logic.

"Did we cover it all?" I asked in a small voice. "We talked about what's going in your life—the youth Christmas party and the sermon. We talked about my life—shopping, friends, babysitting. And now you can feel good about yourself because you brought up Jesus. I think it's all complete." I swallowed.

Alexander took his time to reply. When he did, he spoke slowly and cautiously. "For now, sure. If ever you want to know my opinion on why Jesus died, let me know. And if you find yourself considering how Fahada's death can be redeemed, I have a few thoughts on that too."

I pursed my lips, but Alexander continued. "And as for right now, I'm just sorry for pushing you to consider these topics too soon. Will you forgive me?"

Against my will, I softened slightly. "Thank you for apologizing. At least you've learned how to say sorry over the last few years."

"Yeah," Alexander said. "It's because of what Jesus has done in me. Plus, it helps that I love you."

"Then why did you leave," I asked honestly, "if you love me so much? And then why won't you come back? I still need you, you know. If you were here to help me, maybe I would be recovering better from Fahada's death."

"I think God's trying to get your attention, so He can work on your heart."

I snorted softly. "You and this God thing, Alex. You're so predictable."

"But, it is something for you to think on."

"Oh, totally—we can practice that exercise together." I managed to keep my face straight.

After a moment's pause Alexander chuckled. "Ah, I get it—the thinking part."

My grin popped out of hiding. "And on that note, I'll let you work on those warm-up stretches. Get it—exercise, stretches?" I said, copying my brother's words spoken earlier. "I'll see you at Christmas. You'll be home a week from today?"

"The exact date is yet to be confirmed, but I'll see you when I see you, and not a moment before!"

And just like that, our conversation was over.

Setting the phone down, I shook my head slowly. Really, what a boy! He had this habit of noticing my tender spots and pointing them out. Sometimes, it made me feel loved. Other times, the experience felt painful.

Then, there was the God thing. Woodlynd had to be right on this one. The God I called out to on Fahada's behalf—be it just once—had breached my trust. I couldn't be wrong to say that God, if real, enjoys poking at my wounded places and testing my limits. Wouldn't He know that I couldn't handle any more broken relationships? Surely, He would have understood that, piled all together, my father's abandonment, my brother's departure, and Fahada's death would bring me to my knees. Maybe this was exactly what He wanted. I shook my head at the unfairness of the situation.

A solid knock resounded on the door before Mom stepped in. Her eyes passed over my face before locking on the home phone, which lay on my bed's rumpled blankets. "Take that with you as you come down; it's time to set up for supper."

I pressed pause on my considerations and followed Mom down the stairs.

"Are you okay? You seemed pretty agitated with Alexander earlier," Mom said, hand gliding over the bronze-glazed rail.

"No worries. I'm alright."

"Already? You sure?"

My eyebrows drew together as I stared at the back of Mom's head. "Yeah, why?"

Mother drew in a deep breath, but the exhale lasted longer.

"You're so much like your father that way."

Now I was thoroughly confused. "What do you mean? What way? How do I remind you of Uncle Dallas?"

Mother halted at the bottom of the stairs and faced me. "I'm not referring to Dallas, I'm referring to Drew, your dad."

I blinked. I couldn't remember the last time she had brought up my dad, never mind referred to him by his first name.

Mom peered into my face. Now that she had something to say, she was going to say it, leaving no detail blurry. And whatever she had to say, she wanted my complete attention.

"Your dad was an emotional roller coaster at times—just like you. At the very least, he was a bit unpredictable. At first I found that fascinating." She cleared her throat. "Obviously, something changed."

I broke Mom's stare, not wishing her to read the feelings tumbling through my eyes. Maybe this was why Mom always favored Alexander over me. Alexander was more predictable and stable, whereas every time I revealed my emotional intensity, it would dig deep into Mom's painful memories with Dad.

My dad. I tried not to remember, but all I could do was remember. Oh, how I loved the way Daddy would pick me up and spin me around—ever so tenderly. How I loved when he would brush the hair from my face and kiss my cheek—ever so tenderly. How I loved our late-night cuddles, especially the times he took me outside to view the stars. And then he would call me his starlight.

My head spun. "Is that why you're so closed off to me? Because of him?"

I looked up again. Now it was I who attempted to read every slight change in her expression.

Mom held my gaze. "I'm sorry."

The sincerity of those two simple words caught me off guard. "Why? Why are you sorry? What happened?"

I hardly knew how to ask the questions that burned inside of me: Why did my daddy leave? What motivated him to leave behind his 'starlight'? Where could I place the blame of his abandonment? What should I feel? Each question pounded against my head. I knew a headache was about to grab hold.

"I'm sorry because it was me who asked Drew to leave. And, yes, he's why I'm so closed off to you."

The direct words stabbed deep, even though they struck me as true. Why else would my daddy leave me? What else could motivate him to leave behind his starlight?

"How? Why? What destroyed your relationship?"

Mom sighed. "This is a long story, and I'm not sure I want to delve into it now."

Because of me, right? I wanted to ask. The fact that she didn't feel close enough to me to share her heart pressed on some tender spot in me.

When I didn't let her off the hook, she continued. "I

have my own woundedness, you know."

My eyes narrowed. The same response happened internally as I weighed and sifted through her words warily.

Mom picked up on my reaction and chuckled quietly. "You're so easy to read, Ari. Your thoughts are all over your face. The worst of it is, I know you're right. My own broken past isn't a good enough excuse for why I closed myself off to him—and, later on, to you." Mom chewed her lower lip for a moment. "I could've poured into him, Ariela. I could've loved him. I could've appreciated him. Sure, maybe he was never the perfect match for me, but we still could've had a better marriage. I guess I was just never satisfied with what I had. And now…it seems all I have is taken from me. First my son." Mom reached for my hand. "And now my daughter is pushing herself away too. And the worst of it is, the only one I can blame for this mess is myself."

Mom wrung her hands. "Ha, you can tell I've been doing a lot of thinking lately, hey? I don't even know what to do with all these thoughts." Mom looked up at me again. "And now those walls are going over your eyes. You don't know whether to trust me or not."

My jaw tensed further. Mom's verbalized, blunt observations ran over my protective shield like acid, revealing to me how vulnerable I really was.

Mom's face softened and she stopped wringing her hands. Instead, she said, "I know what you need," and engulfed my stiff body in a motherly hug. "I don't want to push you away like I did your father," she whispered gently. "I never want you to feel like leaving me is a relief. Sweetheart, I want to learn how to have a proper relationship with you."

Good luck hypocrite, were the words clinging to the tip

of my tongue. I struggled to keep myself calm and cool. On one hand, I felt loved. On the other hand, I was afraid. Afraid that it wouldn't last. Afraid that if I learned to become vulnerable with my mother, she would reject me. Afraid.

Against my will, I soaked into my mother's arms. I guess if she was willing to hug me, I might as well submit. At least, that is how I rationalized my need for my mother's love.

While outwardly I collapsed in her arms, inwardly I resisted desperately. If I had trusted both Dad and Alexander to protect me and stay by my side, but they left, how could I trust this aloof and mysterious woman who could sear off my protective sheen with a single phrase? Who only asked for a closer relationship with me when the one with her son could not be furthered? Was this not why she was hugging me now, just because Alexander was not here to take it?

I shut my eyes against the pain of confusion and rejection roiling about in my mind. It's painful to be weak.

Mom released me. "Come. Let's put some food in our tummies. Your uncle has been concocting a stir fry, if my nose interprets correctly."

I just wished it was my daddy in the kitchen.

Even Uncle Dallas was grim as we ate. I knew he must have overheard. As a matter of habit, I pulled up my knees and rested my plate on top.

"Ari—you know I love you, right?" It was Uncle Dallas.

"Could I be excused from the table?" I pushed the chair back from the table and stood up, plate in hand. "I've gotta go study."

"I do love you."

I nodded, hoping he could see the shine of tears in my eyes. To see that I was hurting, but that he shouldn't push. I hoped he would recognize that I did know he loved me. Just that he didn't love me like my daddy did.

All these thoughts I mulled on as I tramped up to my room. I set my plate on the cracked tile floor and froze. There, slid between my mattress and my bed-stand, was the box Fahada had given me. The box of treasures that I had never dared to open. Swallowing hard, I tore my gaze away and crawled into my bed. My heart thumped against my chest and I stared straight ahead. Maybe now was the time to open the box. It felt like an urn to me—an unwelcome reminder of death. Maybe...maybe Woodlynd would help me explore the mysterious "treasures" from Fahada's container.

I checked my phone for mail and skimmed over the lone message. My lips puckered. It wasn't Woodlynd.

It was Lilac, wanting to know how I was doing. Simple as that. This was her third attempt to get a hold of me. She had already left a message on both my cell phone and at the home number. The latter I had deleted before my mom or uncle could listen to it and pass it on to me. I wasn't ready then.

I tilted my head. I was already feeling vulnerable and exposed—at least if I talked with Lilac, I would no longer feel alone.

Maybe she could help me with the box.

My fingers fell on the phone's keypad to form a response, but the words wouldn't come. Frustration gripped me at my inability. Nothing in life came easy. How I wished it was over.

Skip it; I'll just phone her.

Before I had the time to change my mind, I dialed.

Lilac answered the phone immediately. "Hi, Lilac speaking."

"Hey, Lilac, this is Ariela. Got a moment?"

"Well, I can sure make a moment, Ariela!" Lilac said without hesitation. "Did you get my text? Or my messages? I haven't seen you for the last four weeks!"

I bowed my head slightly, too embarrassed to reply.

Lilac slowed down her words. "Moral of the story, I'm missing you, girly."

The words gathered in my throat, but, somehow, I couldn't form my reply.

Lilac waited for a moment, listening even to my silence. Still, she spoke before I could. "What's on your heart? Make yourself cozy if you'd like, 'cause I've got time. I haven't heard a lot from you recently. I feel like you've disappeared off the map since our friend died." We both knew who 'our friend' was. "Why did you call?"

My unhappy thoughts buzzed around my head. My stomach rumbled, but I didn't want the rest of my food. "Fahada was such a cheerful one," I said. "I rarely saw her down; she just always would spring back so fast. And when my mind was full of chaos, she was the only one who could talk over it."

"Some friends are irreplaceable, huh?"

I nodded emphatically. "Lilac, I miss Fahada. Could you do me a favor? Could you just," I briefly halted midsentence, "just talk?"

Lilac didn't laugh, to my relief.

"Now that Fahada's gone there's no one around to speak over the noise of my own thoughts. I'd like to have that back again." I chuckled at the irony. "Her rambling used to drive me insane! Now here I am, literally asking for someone to talk! What do you think Fahada would have to say to me right now?"

While she considered, I crawled onto my window seat, fluffing up a pillow to fill the hollow of my back.

"I—I'm not Fahada," Lilac said.

I imagined Lilac nibbling her lower lip as she tried to pull out an answer.

"I really don't know what she'd say. Maybe, she'd suggest going out for ice cream?" Lilac said.

The corners of my mouth drooped. "That's okay," I said. "Fahada was one of a kind. She was always like that." I breathed in deeply, forcing a slight smile to cling onto my face. "I could sure do with one of her Oh Henry bars right now! She always used to keep a stash of chocolate in her purse."

Lilac smacked her lips loudly. "Sounds like a good friend to me!"

"She had every type of chocolate you've ever heard of—she kept it on rotation which ones she carried in her purse. The girl always had Oh Henry's, though—none of the others performed the same chemical reaction in me, it seems."

Lilac laughed. "That's some interesting medicine."

"Oh yeah. It did it every time." I took a deep breath. "She was a good friend," I said.

"Too bad she's not here wielding chocolate bars, eh?" Lilac said softly. "It's okay to miss her. Do you think of her often?"

A sudden wave of guilt swept over me. I wanted to answer, 'yes'. I lowered my tone to say, "I don't think about her as much as I should. Sometimes... I forget."

I could envision Fahada's face before me: smiling, cheerful, a tad bit mischievous. I could almost hear the last words she had spoken to me, "I am going to tell my brother tonight." Tears started to spill involuntarily down onto my cheeks. Why hadn't I stopped her? Why? I knew something felt wrong!

The familiar dark haze fell over my eyes. "It was my fault. My fault that she died."

I hated those words. I wish I could snatch them from the air, retrieve them from the phone's receiver, and erase them from the invisible chalkboard. Or materialize the words and rip them into shreds like I had done with Lilac's Bible. Lilac's Bible.

"My fault for so many things," I mumbled.

"What's going on, Ariela?" Calm as always, Lilac expected an answer.

Something clicked, and my bitterness seized me, spilling over into my words. "I fell into a deep sleep of delightful dreams as my dad drove away one last time. Instead of supporting Alexander's dreams I let him leave, knowing that every step away gave me a jolt of pain. And, I knew, instinctively knew, that something was very wrong when Fahada planned to announce her conversion to Jawid. I could've set my foot down. I knew I should have said something to change her mind!"

"I know this is hard. I know how you feel. But, maybe it's time to let go, and seek healing instead of remorse."

I shook my head, sending the brimming tears flying across my face. "You don't know me, Lilac. Not like you think you do." Images flooded my mind of the terrible night. The stilled heart monitor. Shreds of Bible pages scattered across the floor. Bright stars glaring at me accusingly from the night sky. Faces flashing before my eyes of people I would never see again—Daddy, Fahada.

"What more can God take from me?" I asked.

Swallowing my tears, I planted my face deep into my

bed. My cries were muffled in the pillow. I wished that I could die there, like that. Suffocated. Vacant. Like Fahada—dead. But, unlike Fahada, I was still afraid to die. A few moments later I pushed myself up from the pillow, breathing heavily.

"Ariela!" The sound from my cell was muted, coming from a hand's reach away.

Why did I call her anyway? She's just making it worse. I stared blankly at the screen of my phone casting a hazy glow on my face. A fuzzy memory slipped into my mind. A different time I'd been staring blankly at that same screen—and the text message there, the message that directed me to the hospital. My fingers trembled. I wanted to throw the thing against the wall. I wanted to scream. I wanted to scream, 'I hate myself!'

"I'm here, I'm here," I said, snatching the phone to my ear. "Listen, I'm glad I called, but I think it's time we wrapped this up."

"Could I just say one thing, Ariela?"

I let a sigh slip through my teeth. "What could it hurt."

"Ariela, you mourn like someone who has no hope."

I blinked, taken aback. Lilac's statement flew in the face of Woodlynd's claim that he was enough to pull me through. With narrowed eyes I prepared to assess her words. "So," I said, "what do you suggest?"

"You know that Bible I gave you?"

As Lilac's words rose with excitement, as if she were about to usher me into her world, my heart sank. I glanced down as if to avoid her eyes. "Yep, I remember it."

Lilac rushed along in her gentle sort of way. "Jesus can give you a hope like Fahada's: a dream and a vision that you know will come true. Seek and you will find. Why don't you do some research?"

I grimaced. "I've already found someone to carry me through, Lilac," I said, attempting to sound nonchalant yet confident. "And, besides, it's Christmas break. Are you asking me to study during the holidays?" I teased.

"You're sure?" Lilac asked, her built-up enthusiasm deflating word by word. "What about the Bible? What have you read already?"

I shook my head, finding it hard to believe that she was actually waiting for a legitimate answer. I chewed a little more on my lower lip, biding time. She could have asked a different question. Tension gathered in my body like the growing rumbles of a thunderstorm. My sigh was like the accompanying wind. "I don't have your Bible anymore. On the day Fahada died, I threw it out," I said. "As a mess of torn pages," I added a little quieter. I briefly shut my eyes and swallowed, all the while fighting the warmth spreading across my face. "It wasn't meant as an act of spite against you. But, it was meant as a slap in Jesus' face… if His face hasn't already rotted in the grave." I swallowed my excess saliva once again. "I can't seriously believe Jesus would appreciate a half-hearted inspection of His precious words, when I've already found the answer. And a half-hearted 'so sorry'? No way would He even want that."

"Do you want me to answer, or are you just commenting?" Lilac said gently. I knew that if she were in person, her hand would be resting on my shoulder as she waited.

"Go ahead."

Lilac inhaled a deep breath and let it out with a thoughtful sigh. "I noticed your apprehension about Jesus' resurrection. You don't know if Jesus is even alive, but do you know what? He knew and loved you before you were born. At your birth He had already eagerly penned each day in the story of your life. He's a Storyteller."

I angled my face to the side, a picture of a feather pen flying across a papyrus scroll flitting through my mind. I imagined candlelight casting a glow on the paper and shadows across the young Father's face. When the candle flickered just right, one could notice the soft and growing smile. Every now and then, He would cast a glance to the left, where a newborn girl lay at rest in her cradle. I blinked suddenly, forcing this picture of God off my mental screen.

Lilac continued, "Even if your mother could forget you as a nursing baby or your father would heartlessly reject you, the LORD will remember and receive you. You ripped his Word to bits, but He will take the broken pieces of your heart and mend them."

Just like how Daddy used to patch up my skinned knees before planting a silly, sloppy kiss on my cheek? I attempted to shove the memory away, but it sucked me deeper instead. My face would wrinkle as I wiped away the slobber, but one look in my father's face would release a smile that reversed my face's ripples. Then Dad would train me anew. The time I biked alone and hurt myself, the sincerity of my father's tone as he reprimanded me caused me to never copy the mistake again.

Lilac's voice mellowed further and her words slowed. "Ripping up God's message to you was like the slap in Jesus' face the soldiers gave Him on the day He died for you; yet if you accept Him, He will wipe every tear from your eye on the day you enter His life. And you know what else, Ari? He's ready to forgive you, too."

I knew instinctively to resist, yet by now my soul was in too reflective and soft a state. "So," I said, drawing out the word, "you're not mad about what happened to your

Bible?"

"No, Ari, that's not my main concern. My main concern is that you understand—" for a moment Lilac's tongue fumbled for the right word. "All good things originally come from God. Let me be blunt for a moment here," Lilac pleaded, "in Hell, there will be no gifts from God. There will be no good, only evil, darkness, and pain."

I'm sure fear darted through my eyes as I blocked the images of leaping flames enveloped in darkness—my imagined hell. Obviously, the choice between Jesus or not held more in the balance than I had expected.

Oblivious to my thoughts, Lilac plowed on, sincerity seeping into her words. "On earth, though, it's harder to differentiate between good and evil, since God's gifts are everywhere. Don't just pick what appears good; pick what is for sure the best."

Emerald green eyes flashed through my mind. *Woodlynd.* Or was Jesus really the best? She said "for sure." How could I know for sure? The question's implications loaded my mind, while its urgency seeped into my mind's cracks. My head bowed like a reed. For a brief instant I wondered if the mental weight imposed actual physical pressure.

"Okay," I said.

"Okay?" Lilac prodded. "What do you mean by that?"

"I mean I'll think about it," I said, sliding off my bed. "There's another reason why I called, Lilac. I need help with something—to open a gift Fahada gave me. You up for it?"

"You bet I am!"

"Great, let me just get it out," I said, lifting the box out of its dusty home.

"Actually," Lilac hesitated, "Maybe that would be

91

something better to do in person. I have studying to do tonight for classes, so could I pop by your house this week? Say, Thursday at seven o'clock PM?"

I dropped the box, letting it hit the ground with a solid thump. I was silent for a moment. "Sure, let's do it."

Chapter 13

I Will Remember

A rush of smoke shot up toward the night sky as loudly crackling flames engulfed the logs. Woodlynd shook out his mittens, now covered in bark chips. He settled himself down on the log next to mine, his arm reaching for my shoulders.

I glanced toward the patio door, wondering when Tiffany and Steven would step out with the promised mugs of hot chocolate.

"Don't the stars look so beautiful tonight?" Woodlynd asked in a low voice.

I smirked, the remark striking me as too typical to be romantic. Though the setting was perfect, my mood wasn't right for romance. Snippets from yesterday's conversation with Lilac still stuck to me more than the wood chips did to Woodlynd's mittens.

"Woodlynd, do you remember what you said earlier? How do you think our relationship would change if I considered Jesus?"

Woodlynd's grip around my shoulders tightened as he leaned over to whisper in my ear. "What does that have to do with tonight?"

I shifted to face him, peering intently to catch his gaze

through the faded light. "I'm asking it tonight, that's how."

The patio door swung open. The light of the fire was just enough to illuminate Steve and Tiff's figures as they slipped out of the house, whispering softly to each other.

Woodlynd sighed. "Okay," he said, a hint of irritation lining his voice. "I'll answer."

I cringed at his loud voice. Surely Steve and Tiff had overheard him. This time it was me who leaned closer. "Honestly, though," I whispered. "How would you react?"

"As long as our relationship is priority over your religion, I don't care what you believe." Woodlynd reached out to grab two mugs off the tray Tiff held and passed one to me.

"Thanks, I said, warming my hands on the mug. I breathed deeply to inhale a chocolatey whiff, but, instead, a sudden gust of wind caused smoke to burn all the way up my nostrils. As I coughed, I realized the implications of Woodlynd's words. Woodlynd didn't want my thoughts or my beliefs. But, he did care about my attention. Was that all he wanted? I shot a glance at his face.

"Are you okay?" Woodlynd laid his hand on my knee, rubbing circles as my last cough resonated throughout the yard.

"All good," I lied. My resigned, thoughtful voice reminded me of Fahada's, when she explained to me her fear of death. Was it just the next day that she confidently commanded me, "Never forget: Jesus is worth it always"?

"I will remember," I whispered.

"What's that?" Woodlynd peered at my face, brow furrowed.

"Just talking to myself," I said.

I readjusted the cup in my hands and took a sip. As the warm liquid glided down my throat, I closed my eyes and asked Jesus to show me if He truly was the Living God. When I opened my eyes, I noticed how beautiful the stars were. *Could they be a gift from God to me?*

By the time Woodlynd dropped me off at quarter to eleven that evening, it wasn't the stars on my mind anymore. I opened my curtains to gaze after his car as the headlights faded into the darkness. I collapsed onto my bed, as the day, too, faded into the night.

*   *   *

Tuesday, November 29th

"Good morning, Sissy!"

I bolted upright and screamed simultaneously with shock.

My sleep-filled, blurry eyes gradually returned to a seeing-capable state. I spun my head from side to side as the morning light streamed out around me.

My eyes narrowed as they fixed on the young man stepping closer, and closer. With tousled brown hair and stubble lining his jaw, he appeared strikingly familiar.

For a moment I froze. Gradually, a smile stretched across my face. Pulling myself out of my bed with a hint of hesitancy, I wagged my finger at him. "Next time, don't you be going about scaring me like that!"

Alexander stuck his tongue out at me.

My. Brother. Is. Standing. Right. In. Front. Of. Me. No. Way!
My whole body tingled.

"Alexander," I said, impulsively wrapping my arms around my beloved brother in a big, squishy hug. "Back so soon?" It felt so good to be in my brother's arms again.

"It was a last-minute plan, actually."

The way Alexander so nonchalantly said that made me suspicious. Taking a step back, I gave him my best fake glare. "Look me in the eye, Alex. Something smells fishy, and this time I don't think it's your armpits."

Alexander snorted.

"You know what I'm talking about, don't you? Spit out why you're here, or you'll regret it! I've grown some big muscles since you've seen me last," I said, flexing my right arm.

"Well, two reasons, really," Alexander said slowly, letting the words roll around in his mouth.

"Tell me the one you were going to say second."

"No. Patience is a virtue, Sis!"

I shoved a finger close to his face in playful defiance. "So is kindness."

Alexander ignored me stubbornly. "Firstly, Pastor Garth gave me permission to spend a few days with you guys as a surprise present."

"You think it's a present to scare your sister half to death?" I mumbled with a smirk. "So? What's the other reason?" I said a little louder.

"Well, there's this young woman—"

I grabbed Alexander's shoulder eagerly. "That's more like it! And what's her name?"

"Lilac."

"Lilac?" I froze. Barely a muscle twitched when I added breathlessly, "The ice cream Lilac?"

"You know when you introduced me to her the day before I left? I realized that she would make an amazing mentor for you. So, I left early the next morning to talk to her—"

"Alexander!" I exclaimed, no longer frozen.

"What?"

"That is so, so sweet!"

"Yeah." He smirked. "The ice cream contained a lot of

sugar, as usual."

I rubbed my face in exasperation, but couldn't help smiling. "And?"

"And... I asked her to stay in contact with you and to let me know how you're doing via phone call. But, eventually... eventually our discussions grew longer. And they weren't just about you anymore," Alexander conceded.

I just stared at him, mouth slightly agape. Suddenly, I knew for sure what he was getting at. Was this really, really happening?

Alexander tilted his head to peer into my face. "Are you okay? I mean, I thought you'd be happy when you heard that we're dating."

"You're dating?" I shrieked, and again flung my arms around him and squeezed until I heard something pop.

"Ooh, much better." Alexander said. "You put my back into place again."

"This is official? You're actually dating Lilac? This is a match made in Heaven, I tell you! Of course, I'm happy, I'm overjoyed! I'm—"

Alexander smirked. "I get the point. Anyway, someone drove here with me and I need to drop her off."

The door creaked open and Lilac's face peeked in.

I flew over and embraced her. It was a good day to hug.

*   *   *

The gusting wind sent strands of my hair every which way. I pulled it all back into a pony tail using the band on my wrist.

I glanced at Alexander as he tramped along beside me, hands in his pockets, but all I saw of his face was a mass of that tousled hair. Unlike me, he didn't bother to sweep it back and out of the way.

The breakfast our whole family had devoured together just half an hour before—the first time in a long time—tossed and turned in my stomach as I hurried to match my brother's long strides. I had forgotten that boiled eggs didn't sit well with me.

"Let me get this," Alexander said over the wind. "This was the first time you told Mom and Dad about your boyfriend?"

I nodded sheepishly. At breakfast Alexander had asked just the right question, in just the right way. I had admitted that there indeed was a special someone in my life.

"So, are you going to follow their suggestion and invite him over for a meal sometime soon?" Alexander questioned.

"I don't know," I mumbled. The cold wind puffed my words away.

"You get it that you're not supposed to keep dating him until then, right?" Alexander said. I didn't understand how his voice could be heard so easily over the noise.

"I know," I shouted loudly. My voice carried over the wind, but it also carried with it a lot of pent up frustration. "Maybe I won't date him at all," I shouted again. "Could we change the subject?"

"Sure," Alexander said slowly, clearly stunned by my last remark.

I paused awkwardly for a moment. I spat a hair out of my mouth and plowed forward, without transition. "I've been thinking, Fahada sure seemed pretty confident that to sacrifice for Jesus was no big deal, even that He was worth all she could give." I let my words hang there, without completion. I shoved my ungloved fingertips into my pant pockets. "I mean, she never really met Jesus."

"But, Jesus' twelve apostles did," Alexander said. "And, I am, as Fahada was, confident that they met the risen Jesus too. They gave up their lives because they believed the carpenter from Bethlehem rose from the grave." Alexander paused to zip his sweater higher. I took the opportunity to do the same with my winter coat. "Ari," he said, catching my eye, "would you be willing to die and be tortured for a lie? But, countless of ancient letters and writings have confirmed that Jesus' disciples did die for their beliefs. And, do you know what else?" Alexander's strides seemed to grow longer and faster as I scurried to keep up. This time, I hung on every word, begging the wind not to steal any of them away. Alexander continued, hands out of his pockets and alive with gestures. "Five hundred people claimed to see Jesus after He rose from the dead. Five hundred people can't be permanently hypnotized all at once! Even if they were hallucinating, they wouldn't have all had the same hallucination. You have to consider the option, Ari... I mean, this is the same Being who created balls of burning gas in the sky and placed them in a perfectly timed rotation, so that in 2 B.C., Jupiter—the King Planet—and Venus—the Mother Planet—would cross paths to form the Christmas star above a lonely stable. Is it not possible that this same Being could raise His Son from death to life?"

"What you said about that star," I stammered, "is that confirmed?"

Alexander shrugged. "Just ask NASA."

I stopped in my tracks. "Are you saying that actually happened?" I shook the cobwebs out of my head. "I mean, that it's actually scientifically proven?"

My brother turned to face me. The sincerity in his face struck me as uncharacteristically intense. "Well, that's what

NASA's technology shows; Google it. The point is, this isn't the kind of God you want to mess with. But, He is the kind of God who would remove the sting from death—and He did, by raising Jesus Christ from the dead to foreshadow our life after death! That is, foreshadowing our life and joy with God after death if we make room for God in our lives. And, eventually, you've gotta make a choice about this God."

A muddy car zoomed past, reminding me to keep moving. As I stepped forward, Alexander lightly touched my sleeve. "Sis," he said, "God loves you. Please don't forget that, Ari."

I pursed my lips. No, not as a sign that I was about to tune out his words; I pursed my lips in the vain attempt to keep the tears from running down my face. Within moments my eyelids were weighted with mini, sparkling icicles.

"Doesn't the Bible say that Jesus will one day wipe the tears from our eyes? But what if it's winter and they freeze to your eyelashes?" I said, finishing off my tease with a loud snuffle.

God loves me, I thought to myself, before suggesting we return to the house.

*　　　*　　　*

I flicked the light on in my room and made a beeline for my first closet. Reaching up high, I grabbed a small, clear container and brought it down to eye level. I peered inside and sighed. No chocolate.

I tossed it back in its place and instantly stepped toward my hiding spot for Fahada's treasure box. *Should I wait for Lilac?* With a quick tug the ribbon holding the carboard box shut was untied and the flaps popped open. A large, leather-bound book rested snugly within the confines of the cardboard walls. My heart rate accelerated and I ran back to make sure my door was locked. It was. Resting against my bed frame, I flipped the box upside down and allowed the book to slide into my hand. Reverentially, I lifted the cover—only to find a strikingly familiar face staring back at me. The face didn't perfectly match the person—it was an artist's rendition. My gut clenched. My eyes were locked on the smiling face of Jawid.

Smiling? Why smiling?

Jawid's hand lifted high a sort of stringed instrument, though it wasn't a guitar. I spotted writing at the bottom of the page, but the messy words were in another language—maybe Arabic.

I released a pent-up breath and forced myself to turn the page. Jawid was there again—this time with Fahada at his side as the one grasping the instrument. Jawid's face was soft with tenderness.

I slammed my fist against his figure. "No," I said. "No! Jawid isn't kind. Jawid didn't give Fahada gifts. Jawid hated her! Jawid..." But Fahada's grin, sketched by her own hand, stopped me short.

There was a date written on this page. This picture was drawn only a couple months before Fahada joined my school. I kept flipping through the thick, creamy pages of the sketchbook, discovering a side of Fahada I had never known. I landed upon a startlingly realistic picture of myself that made me laugh. I found a couple more pictures of Jawid, but one in particular caught me off guard. The bags beneath Jawid's eyes were dark as he stared at a large book open before him. This started an alarming series of drawings as Jawid's facial expressions progressed from sad, to angry, to completely blank and distant.

I'm afraid, Fahada had written at the bottom of one page. I shuddered. *This* was the Jawid I knew. I shut the book slowly and breathed deeply.

What would I find next? Was I ready to see?

I found my spot and flipped the page to find a group of people lined up on Fahada's bed. Jawid sat straight and tall, holding a large book high above his head. There was me, mouth as round as the letter "O", but empty handed. And there was Lilac, pointing to the lines of a book open on her lap. Fahada merely stood facing them, hands spread across the top of her head.

I shifted uncomfortably, wishing Fahada had drawn me comforting her. Had I been no help to her? I quickly moved on.

The colours of an aurora borealis lighted the next page, while two human shadows stretched across it. The shadows were dancing with each other. *Jesus delights in me,* Fahada's calligraphy pen had recorded. From that page on, the theme of Fahada's sketchbook was different, completely changed. It was centered on Jesus. Page after page... all about Jesus.

Soon I encountered a painting, rather than a drawing. In it, a glossy river cascaded from a golden throne. The smiling King reached out His hand toward a kneeling girl—a kneeling girl with the long flowing hair characteristic to Fahada.

I shook my head slowly. Was this King *really* the One Fahada wanted more than anything and anyone else? Maybe she truly did think that Jesus was worth it.

I turned the page, but it was blank. I flipped to the next, but there was nothing on it. A quarter of the large book had yet been untouched. I stretched out on the floor and rested my cheek against a blank page. My body began to shake, but the tears didn't come.

"God," I said, "in taking my friend to Heaven, You gave her exactly what she longed for."

I was quiet for a long time, breathing in the scent of paper and paint. "Thank You for that. You gave her what I couldn't." Regret swept over me as I whispered those words. "I tried. I truly tried to be the best friend she could get. I tried to put her above Woodlynd. I tried to offer her comfort. Yet You were the One who made the difference, not me." I rolled over onto my back and stared at the ceiling. "Would You want me, too?" I asked, shrugging my shoulders and lifting my arms in the "W" position. "I want to build on the foundation Fahada had, the Foundation that gave her peace."

I shut my eyes tightly. *What am I saying? What kind of Being am I addressing? Isn't this a murderer of the young? Isn't this a tyrant king I am talking to?* In my confusion, the tears rolled down my cheeks.

"No!" I said forcefully. "*That* character is not the God Fahada, Alexander, or Lilac worship. The God of Fahada, Alexander, and Lilac is a God of peace, a God of resolve, and a God of love." I cleared my throat and straightened up to a sitting position, plowing ahead before I could change my mind. "God, I want the peace that Fahada had. I want the confidence that Alexander has. I want the love Lilac has." I inhaled, letting serenity flow in with the air. "I want to follow the God who aligns the planets. Right now... I promise myself to You. I'm Yours." I laughed nervously. "Is that kind of what you're supposed to say, Jesus? I'm sorry for being stubborn and making a mess of my life, and, well, I'll just say it—for sinning." My heart thumped as a new apology came to mind. "I'm sorry for seeking Woodlynd instead of seeking You. I'm sorry for making a human my god, when You're the true Master of this life. I can't promise myself to someone who isn't promised to You." My heart sank even as I spoke. "You wouldn't ask me to give him up, would You? Would You change his heart for me, God?"

I furrowed my brow as if to listen. All I felt was a flood of peace rushing over me, loosening my tight muscles and refreshing my mind. Like a gentle spring rain, God was watering my dying places which were thirsty for love.

I snatched a pen and the sketchbook. My eyes lit up with excitement. "☐☐☐☐☐☐, ☐☐☐☐☐ ☐☐☐☐☐☐ ☐☐☐☐ ☐☐☐☐☐ ☐☐ ☐☐☐☐☐ ☐☐. ☐☐☐☐☐☐."-☐☐☐☐☐☐, I penned. I wrinkled my nose, wishing I had as pretty writing as Fahada.

I hesitated for a moment, then grabbed a different pen, a paper-mate gel pen with sky-blue ink. ☐ ☐☐☐☐ ☐☐☐☐☐☐☐☐, I wrote.

I picked up my ordinary pen once more. "☐☐☐, ☐☐☐ ☐☐☐☐☐ ☐☐☐. ☐☐☐☐☐☐ ☐☐☐'☐ ☐☐☐☐☐☐ ☐☐☐☐, ☐☐☐." - ☐☐☐☐☐☐☐☐☐.

I decorated the page with sky-blue swirls and twirls before penning in bolded letters, ☐ ☐☐☐☐ ☐☐☐☐☐☐☐☐.

Since Jesus laid down his life for me, I could lay down a boyfriend for Him. *Is this what He is asking?* The question clouded my mind like a storm brewing overhead. Alarmed, I flipped back to Fahada's throne-room scene. Soaking in the picture of the King, the clouds in my mind dissipated.

In the place of Fahada I pictured myself and Woodlynd kneeling side-by-side.

I sighed. "Jesus, I know You're worth giving up anything for, but... would you make this a reality instead?"

The distant pitter-patter of rain upon the tin roof lent an atmosphere of harmony to the tiny chapel. I didn't mind that the autumn rain had forced the ceremony inside. Fingering the folds of my bridesmaid gown, I couldn't help but shift slightly from foot to foot as I scanned the room. The coziness of the hundred celebrants removed any unnecessary barriers between the group. The place was full of family.

Speaking of family, I finally spotted her—the friend who would soon become the newest member of mine, eleven months after her relationship with my brother had officially began.

Arms linked with her father, Lilac smiled sweetly at friends and family as she progressed past the aisles. With a final wink to me, she set her adoring gaze on Alexander.

Lilac's father and mother stood there, motionless. The father's cheek suddenly twitched, and his jaw tensed. Compassion flooded through me, plus a sense of deep, aching regret as an unwanted thought occurred to me. *Will my real father walk me up the aisle on my wedding day? Will I even have a wedding day?*

Once, I had dreamed of Woodlynd in Alexander's place

and I as the bride. But, then he had turned his sparkling emerald eyes on Jade—only two weeks after I had told him I needed a break in our relationship to think and pray. I could still feel the warmth in my hand as if he were holding it.

Why do I care? I broke my stare from Lilac's father's shoe and returned my attention to Alexander and Lilac, letting a smile grace my face again.

I smirked internally at my own fallible mind. Woodlynd had gone, but another boyfriend could come. My father had left me, yet my Heavenly Father would never leave me. God was there for keeps.

I had lived my life as a dry fountain—declaring my ugliness, my unlovable nature, my hopeless state from a sand-paper tongue thirsty for love. God sent Lilac to guide me to the Spring of Living Water.

I had been terrified by the hollowness that invaded my most joyful friend. When I couldn't fill in the gaps, she found the Giver of Peace, the One who gives *eternal* peace—unlike me.

Now, Woodlynd, with his flattering attention, was on a page I had already turned; but God had His fingerprints on every page.

This storytelling God was the One I had obeyed, the One I had said "yes" to. As the Source of my life and my Reward for eternity, He was redeeming my story and trading my ashes for a crown of beauty. I no longer needed to look to my dad, Fahada, or Woodlynd for a happy ending.

And somewhere else inside, I heard the words I had longed to hear for the last nine years, "My starlight, I will never leave you nor forsake you."

My Daddy had come for me.

=Going Deeper Study=

Greetings, beloved keeners!

Enjoy the below sections as a method for personal reflection—or adapt it for group discussion!

HOPE

Many of my greatest joys stem from the relationships in my life. However, relationships can sometimes bring more than joy—they also bring angst and trials. You see, the fact that Ariela often turned back the clock to memories of her father, found joy in Alexander, felt Fahada's pain, noticed tension with her mother, and felt treasured in Woodlynd's presence was not the primary issue in her life. The cause of her problems was where she put her *hope*—and what she expected of whom.

> *"In him our hearts rejoice, for we trust in his holy name. May your unfailing love rest upon us, O LORD, even as we put our hope in you." (Psalms 33:21-22 New International Version)*

Paul tells us that when push comes to shove, only three things should be prioritized: faith in God, hope in God, and love of God. (1 Cor. 13:13) To hope is to desire with expectation of obtainment or fulfillment[1]. God is the One who gives graciously without finding fault, yet still we place our hope elsewhere. The Israelites sought after other unstable nations to save them from their enemies. I tend to place my hope for security in money and personal abilities. Ariela hoped for her earthly relationships to give her the consistent love of a Father.

Pause & Ponder: Where do you place your hope?

I can tell you with confidence that God *does indeed* provide! God is indeed worthy of our hope and a life of trust. Placing our hope in God may look like investing your prayers, obedience, time, or money to pursue something that doesn't make complete sense from the world's perspective.

When Israelite king Hezekiah called upon God for rescue from the army besieging Jerusalem, God answered by destroying an army of 185,000. Yes, the Bible says that the angel of the LORD struck down the whole enemy army in a single night, without the help of any soldiers. Indeed, when God called Gideon to free the Israelites from the tyranny of the Midianites, God kept on insisting on a smaller army. Then, "Gideon's" army of only 300 men wrought havoc on the large united force of the armies of their enemies.

God can provide for us financially too. A silly story from my life was the time I set my heart on buying a certain pair of jeans. We had bought a size too small on a significant sale price but couldn't trade it out at the same price. I wrestled with the decision for some time. Finally, I

[1]Merriam-Webster

felt God asking me to, instead, donate the amount of money I had been hoping to spend on the jeans. Instantly, I felt released. It wasn't much later that I found the exact same pair of jeans at about a quarter of the original price. How perfect! Plus, God has continued to provide for me and answer my prayers with unique work opportunities that fit my current stage of life.

When Ariela submitted her life to Christ, she found her desire for a loving Father satisfied.

Pause & Ponder: Prayerfully ponder how God has provided for you at a time when you chose to place your hope in Him. (See Isaiah 50:30-31)

REMEMBER

I mentioned that in surrender to God, Ariela found a Father. This change of life came about by God's power, yes, but also because Ariela chose to *remember*. In order to make her final conclusion about Jesus, Ariela drew upon Fahada's legacy and her brother's plea.

> *"Why are you downcast, O my soul? Why so disturbed within me? Put your hope in God, for I will yet praise him, my savior and my God. My soul is downcast within me; therefore, I will remember you from the land of the Jordan, the heights of Hermon—from Mount Mizar." (Psalms 42:5-6 NIV)*

Why do we read so many great books, watch so many inspiring movies, and listen to so many interesting sermons, if only to file all that information at the back of our minds? I am amazed at myself that much of the information I've gathered leads to little change. Information contains the potential for change, God holds the power to transform, and we have the responsibility to apply the steps God has given us.

We start with belief—and, of course, what we believe is based upon what we think. "For as he thinks within himself, so he is.[2]" (Proverbs 23:7a, NASB) We can attempt to stop worrying by suppressing our fears...yet we know that if we try to lose weight by no longer eating, the hunger will eventually get to you. Fill up on good thoughts–on God's truth rather than the world's lies. A Lilac-like mentor in my life often advises girls to be persistent in stating truth in our minds. Worry and self-pity divert our attention from the true battle, and insecurity and shame can cripple our ministry. Feelings start with our thoughts and other input, such as media. Therefore, we can combat these attitudes by stating truth: *If God cares for the sparrows, surely, He will provide for me.* Replace self-pity with thanking God for what He's given you. Replace insecurity by reminding yourself that you are created fearfully and wonderfully, and that God prefers to use the unlikely—such as: tiny armies, quiet prayers, teenagers (Mary, the mother of Jesus), and persecutors (Paul the Apostle). Crush shame by reminding yourself that no one can condemn us because it is God who justifies and Christ Jesus—who died and was raised to life—is at the right hand of God interceding for us.

Pause & Ponder: What is a lie, attitude, or tendency that has been plaguing you? Ask Jesus where it started – be it a lie you've been telling yourself, friends who influence you negatively, or the media you soak in.

---

[2]In *Switch on Your Brain* Dr. Caroline Leaf explains this concept in an interesting and scientific fashion.

Listen & Learn: Ask Jesus to remind you of a verse or Biblically-sound principle to combat that lie. Commit to speaking it over yourself each time the issue surfaces. If the problem had more to do with a person, media source, or something else, ask Jesus if there's another step for you to take.

Notice how I suggested asking Jesus for a step of obedience. To me, that's a scary question to ask Jesus! It was scary for Ariela too. Her boyfriend had been drawing her away from God. She wrestled with her desires, sensing that God wanted her to distance herself from Woodlynd. I think it's okay to wrestle! It's also super important to obey, as I need to remind myself. Often times, as with Ariela, God will follow up on our steps of obedience by giving us joy. Isn't it amazing? God rewards us just for giving Him what He deserves anyway! The first step is belief, and the second is obedience.

> *"So do not throw away your confidence; it will be richly rewarded. You need to persevere so that when you have done the will of God, you will receive what he has promised." (Hebrews 10:35-36 NIV)*

I encourage you to continually meditate on how God has come through for you before. Forgetting how God had delivered them kept the Israelites, hindered by their complaining and fear, from entering the Promised Land. Don't ignore how God's been faithful in the past. Build upon others' faith stories and remember God's fulfilled promises so that you may inherit what has been promised.

Above all, don't disregard the central point of the gospel: The God Who created us loves us. He died to redeem us from the mess we've brought on ourselves and restore our relationship with Him.

I draw from these rich truths that you are God's...

TREASURE

You are truly treasured.

> *"The Word was in the world, and though God made the world through him, yet the world did not recognize him. He came to his own country, but his own people did not receive him. Some, however, did receive him and believed in him; so he gave them the right to become God's children. They did not become God's children by natural means, that is, by being born as the children of a human father; God himself was their Father." (John 1:10-13 Good News Translation)*

God valued you enough to painfully sacrifice His life in heaven *and* His life on earth. Why? So that you could become His child. How? By believing in Him. This passage isn't mildly referring to simply recognizing Jesus as a truth-teller, but more like putting your hope—expectation, desire, and investment—in Him. Soak in the following verses about being treasured by God.

> *"God decided in advance to adopt us into his own family by bringing us to himself through Jesus Christ. This is what he wanted to do, and it gave him great pleasure." (Ephesians 1:5 New Living Translation)*

> *"For God chose to save us through our Lord Jesus Christ, not to pour out his anger on us. Christ died for us so that, whether we are dead or alive when he returns, we can live with him forever." (1 Thessalonians 5:9-10 NLT)*

"You hear, O LORD, the desire of the afflicted; you encourage them, and you listen to their cry, defending the fatherless and the oppressed, in order that man, who is of the earth, may terrify no more. (Psalm 10:17-18 NIV)

Pause & Ponder: Is it easy or hard for you to understand—and especially accept—God's great love for you? Here's a challenge. Search for at least two more verses that support the point that you are treasured by God. (Hint: What was the verse that helped lead Fahada to Christ?)

We don't need to live in fear of God or people. We know that God loves us. However, we do need to remember that God is also ruling as a holy Judge. Let's not forget that God died for our yuck and sins. One of His many reasons for placing us on earth is to mold our character to be more like His. (Romans 8:29) I believe God will do this both gradually and graciously. Let's partner with Him in this process! Let's set becoming like Him as our hope! (1 John 3:2-3). This is a belief and action combo.

Christianity is a matter of putting "money" where your mouth is—investing in the One we say we put our hope in. It's a matter of dwelling on the One most worthy of our attention and letting His Word take root in our heart as we spend time memorizing and stating His truths. Also, it's a matter of daring to love and be loved. As Jesus laid down His life for us, we can drop our lives in His hand, loving back by obedience, sharing our faith, and passing on His mercy. Ooh...so many ways to grow!

Pause & Ponder: Is it harder for you to: a) invest in your faith sacrificially; b) let the Biblical perspective balance the thoughts in your mind, or; c) receive Jesus' love? Ask Jesus how you can prioritize that aspect in your daily life. Take a simple action step! Perseverance is usually needed for this to stick. I intend to work on these things together with you.

Reflect to Remember: How have the characters in this story impacted you? What can you learn from their roles in this book? First, write down their defining characteristics and a lesson to be learned from them. Then circle the character who *acts* most like you and draw a box around the one you *want* to be most like. Add a verse that best describes the character. Alexander is filled in as an example.

- Alexander – caring, willing to take risks for Jesus, passionate and persistent in sharing his faith; to respect other's feelings while still putting God first (not sacrificing God's call on the altar of people).
  "But speaking the truth in love, we are to grow up in all aspects into Him who is the head, even Christ."
  (Ephesians 4:15 NASB)
- Ariela
- Dallas (Ariela's step-dad)
- Drew (Ariela's dad)
- Fahada
- Lilac
- Marguerite (Ariela's mom)
- Woodlynd
- Any other character you can learn from

Resources for Research

Our faith isn't just a blind faith! Aren't you glad? Ariela's change of faith—or change of hope, I could say—mostly stood upon the transformation she had seen in her friends, yet the scientific reasoning Alexander added in did play a role. In fact, it would be important for Ariela to study and research more as her relationship with God continued. The Bible says that we are to be prepared for every opportunity (Colossians 4:5, 2 Timothy 4:2). We want to defend our faith well, not being caught off guard by questions!

Here are some resources that have either impacted me or have been highly recommended to me.

- *Seeking Allah, Finding Jesus* by Nabeel Qureshi is currently my favourite stand-alone book. In this stimulating read, the author (a Muslim at the story's start) tackles tough questions like the Trinity, divinity of Jesus, and inerrant nature of the Bible.

- *The Case for Christ* movie shares the true testimony of former atheist Lee Strobel and his wife Leslie, covering both the intellectual and emotional types of conversion.

- Books by Lee Strobel

- *On Guard* by William Lane Craig is designed to answer questions like how the universe began, why suffering is in the world, and if Jesus is the Only Way to God—all in a readable fashion.
- ReasonableFaith.org, a website featuring Willliam Craig, is loaded with bite-sized resources.
- *Mere Christianity* by C.S. Lewis is rich with the logic behind our faith, coming from the pen of one of J.R.R. Tolkien's friends.
- *Switch on Your Brain* by Dr. Caroline Leaf is an exciting read which explains the workings of our brain so that we can be better enabled to renew our minds, as the Bible commands.

=Acknowledgments=

I fell in love with fiction first, but it has been my passion for the Bible, God's Holy Word, that began to change me bit by bit. Though daily time in God's Word and prayer are disciplines, to be sure, I treasure both the memories and experiences of many delightful times in God's presence.

Jesus, first, I want to acknowledge *Your* part in this book—and *my* (actually!) miniscule piece in your plan. (Jeremiah 29:11) I am honoured that You would want to include me in Your plan. I am pleased that You asked me to serve You as Your personal apprentice—so that I can use my imagination and writing abilities for something worthwhile. WOW, it is amazing that You would let a little girl like me try my hand at *Your* trade! *Thank You* for faithfully bringing something out of nothing, over and over again! I love You.

Geralyn, I am also so grateful for your mentorship in this writing process. You have gone above and beyond to help me, spending so much time and thought on refining my abilities and helping make my book readable. Thank you for encouraging me to pursue my publishing dreams and for many, many more things, dear cousin!

Mom, you have also contributed to this book by assessing it, encouraging me, and praying for both. Our closeness is a huge treasure and blessing to me. Dad, you are stable, and I appreciate that. I remember notifying you when my book was accepted to be published, and how ecstatic you became. My wonderful brothers, cell leaders, and grandparents—you too have uplifted me in your own ways: whether by acting as excited for my dreams as if they were your own; by hugging me unconditionally; or even by inspiring a character in this story. Know that you are in no way forgotten, but instead held in honor.

There is, of course, one more group of people I'd like to recognize. If you are reading these words right now, you can thank Synecdoche Publishing. Thank you so much, Amanda and your team, for partnering with a novice like me. Your gracious attitude and time dedicated to this project have been noticed and valued.

God, thank you for surrounding me with people like those listed above. May You bless them with what they need in this season in their lives, plus all the readers who flip through these pages. May we, with Ariela, choose to let our lives be changed by remembering the legacy You left and live. Amen!